The Freezer

Kim Hunt

Spiral Collectives

Copyright © 2024 by Kim Hunt

All rights reserved.

No part of this publication may be reproduced, distributed, or transmitted in any form or by any means, including photocopying, recording or other electronic or mechanical methods, without the prior written permission of the publisher except as permitted by U.S. copyright law. For permission requests contact the author.

The story, all names, characters and incidents portrayed in this production are fictitious. No identification with actual persons (living or deceased), places, buildings and products is intended or should be inferred.

Book cover by Biz Hayman Studio.

First edition 2024

Contents

This book is set in Australia.

Always was, always will be

Aboriginal land.

Chapter 1

CAL NYX STOOD ON the rim of the hidden valley, the secret habitat of the Mallemi tree-fern. Across the ravine an aberrant glint of white in the green haze had pulled her vision. Not a slash of ochre from a slip nor a blackened, skeletal bushfire remnant. But a luminous, reflective surface. She scratched her boot through the sandstone rubble as she raised her binoculars. *Some low-life's off-loaded a fridge from the lip of the Lyrebird Track.*

'Fuckin dumpers.'

She resented doing rubbish collection. Not exactly part of her ranger job remit but the local council wouldn't retrieve it on their rounds either. Apart from being an eyesore it was dangerous having an object like that hanging halfway down a cliff. *Why can't people just drop it to the metal recycling at the tip?*

She returned to her truck and started the engine, emptying half a litre of water down her throat before she took off. Spring, and already her air-con was ratcheted to max, combatting the clamminess outside. Cal floored the pedal and rooster-tailed twin sprays of gravel as she headed along the crest.

It took her less than ten minutes to reach the spot. The unsealed roadway, essentially single lane, snaked along the back of the range. Unwise to travel at more than 60kph as there was nowhere to go but down if something appeared from the other direction. That or opt for a head-on. Traffic wasn't much of an issue on a weekday, campers and hikers mostly arrived on the weekends. Still, it only took one vehicle coming her way. Cal parked on a straight length of track visible to any other drivers. They'd have time to stop if not pass her.

She walked back along the trail peering down at the road-edge and below looking for signs. She eventually found the tell-tale angled depression in the crest of gravel and silt at the roadside. The corner of a heavy object had been dropped before being pushed over the edge. Tiny weeds had sprouted in the dent so it had happened more than a couple of days ago. Cal leaned over the crumbling verge, a steep rocky incline that fell hundreds of metres to the valley floor. Gnarly specimens of yellow bloodwood that had sprouted and clawed their roots through the porous sandstone remained clinging to the rock walls. Several of these tenacious survivors had halted the fridge's downward trajectory. She'd have to winch it out.

Cal backed her truck along the ridge and positioned the front with the recovery winch above the spot. Designed to pull her own or another truck out of trouble, a mere freezer wasn't going to strain it any. She dragged a coiled rope, webbing strap and heavy gloves from one of her gear boxes. Tied the rope to the frame under her rear deck. She looped the other end around her waist and knotted it. If she fell and broke a bone help would be a long time coming. She got her satellite phone from the cab and put in a side pocket of her trousers. With the webbing strap over her shoulders she unhooked the wire cable from the winch and ran it out down the side of the bank as she descended, using her gloved hands to slow her. The sun bore directly on her back. The rock face radiated its own stored heat at her front as she shuffled backwards, rocks and grit falling away below her from the unstable surface.

She reached the battered cube and discovered why it hadn't fallen open as it tumbled down the face. The lid was secured with a hasp and padlock. Kinda odd. Maybe someone once stashed their fav Hagen Daas in there and they weren't keen on sharing. She paused and caught her breath, wiping the sweat that was now running into her eyes.

She dragged the webbing strap from her shoulders and worked it around the sides of the box which, on closer inspection, had patches of corrosion and silty soil where the white paintwork had eroded away. Strange to see the soil as the surrounding area was sandstone. It's come from the flats somewhere she surmised. But why does it have soil on it? Was it buried? She fastened the strap-hook then worked the tensioner-handle until it was tight. The broad nylon webbing offered better grip than the wire cable which she attached through the strap where the lid met the main body of the freezer. Satisfied it was all secure, Cal made her slow ascent back up the rock-face.

When she reached the top, she took a breather on the trackside in a thin strip of shade under the pick-up tray. Respite from the sun but her skull still pulsed like an overheated melon in a compost heap. When she'd caught her breath she stood and went to the cab, finished her water.

Standing at the front of the truck, she flipped the lever to operate the winch. The cable pulled taut and Cal leaned over the edge watching as the white cube dragged up the rough bank. When it got to the top she flipped the lever back, pulled her mobile phone, took a picture of the site and the object then logged the GPS details.

She went to another toolbox at the rear of the truck and got a large pry-bar. She righted the freezer to access the hasp and noticed the box was now leaking a dark fluid. It stunk. Like, gag-o-rama. A sickly, revolting stench. She tried to squeeze her throat shut so she wouldn't dry-heave at the fetidness. But still she had to stifle a convulsion in her neck. *They've dumped it and haven't bothered emptying it. Rancid burgers. Nice one.* She worked the pry-bar under the hasp and popped the four screws holding it. Much easier than dealing with the padlock. Then she lifted the lid and immediately fell back with a wave of disgust. She held her hand to her mouth as she gagged, scrabbling backwards away from the sight. She spat and retched to the side, gasping and wiping at her mouth with her sleeve.

'Fuck me.'

In disbelief, she kept her sleeve across the lower part of her face as she crept back for a second look.

A soup of decay and rot and bones. Floating half-submerged in the goop the grotesquery of a rubber gorilla mask, hair and fabricated maw intact. Peeping from beneath that: a human skull.

She dropped the lid, gulping air as she pushed her spine against the side of her truck. She vomited again. Coughing and spitting the contents of her stomach and all the distress that went with the smell and the vision she'd just witnessed. She slid down against the side of her truck, her boot heels scraping back and forth in the gravel. But she remained stationary, not daring to look away from the closed freezer as though the break in her concentration might release some other evil in her direction.

She took several deep breaths and held them low in her diaphragm until her gasping slowed. It was one of those moments when she wished she worked as one of a pair. The only other time that peculiarity occurred to her was when four hands or extra muscular heft was called for. But mostly she figured workarounds for those rare problems. She reached for the sat-phone in her pocket and called her boss, Rod Herring.

'Fisho. Got a strange one. Well another one actually. Becoming a bit of a habit.' She explained her find, reminiscent of a similar horror just months prior.

Herring listened.

'Jesus Cal. You want me to send someone to replace you? Take the day off?'

'Nah. Rather be at work. But thanks.'

'Well, the offer stands. Jeez, how's your luck, or lack of it. You still on The Lyrebird?'

'Yup. Heading for The Valley.' Even among Parks staff the location of the precious tree-ferns was never spoken, not on the airwaves or anywhere else. Those who knew the whereabouts were a small and trusted group. Cal continued.

'I'm gonna call Richmond Police. Guess I'll be waiting here to brief them. Then I'll carry on. Be late when I get there now so I may camp over.'

'Well, if you're sure you're okay there on your own?'

'Yup.'

'Stay in touch. Take care Cal.'

'Will do.' Cal ended the call then used Parks staff access number for direct contact with Richmond Command rather than the direct line to DI Liz Scobie's personal phone which, though tempting, wasn't the right protocol.

She filled in the staffer on the other end and moved to the shade at the rear of her truck. She kept the white refrigerator box in her peripheral vision as she began her wait, clutching her collar to her face to ward of the stench. Unsuccessful.

Chapter 2

CAL HEARD THE WHINE of an approaching diesel-engine from the south-west. Stood and dusted off her uniform. A 4x4 police mini-truck arrived with two male officers in the front seat. One got out from the passenger side, nodded towards Cal and went to the back of the vehicle, withdrawing a pair of bright orange traffic cones. He walked back along the road and placed one cone several metres from the edge of the fallaway. Meanwhile, the driving officer had got out and approached Cal. She recognized him. Buff, blandly handsome. She held out her hand.

'Hello again. Cal Nyx. Parks Service.'

'DS Glen Avery. Met you on the Leuwins case?'

'That's right.' Was Avery being cagey? Cal acknowledged the inquiry six months prior, when she'd found a body in the bush near Boarback Ridge. Turned out to be an old friend of hers and for a time the cops had viewed her as a possible suspect.

'Getting to be a habit, but I just trip over them. Not responsible.' She held her hands up in mock defeat.

She swung her head towards the white freezer near the road-edge as the other office returned from placing the second cone beyond.

'Found it dumped over the side. I spotted it from the other ridge.' She indicated the direction the police had driven from.

'Techs are on their way. This is DC Gavin Hassett,' Avery said.

Hassett was taller than Avery, maybe six foot. Gangly and angular with pocked cheeks. He gave Cal a friendly nod.

'I've tried not to disturb the edge. There's a deep impression where the thing may have been dropped. I had no idea I was gonna find ... whatever that is in there,' Cal grimaced. 'You need me to stick around? Got a bit of a hike inland to get to.'

'We've got your details at Richmond.' Avery had pulled his notebook. 'Last time you would've checked this area? Any way we could get a fix on when it was dumped?' he said.

'My rounds are fairly regular. I only saw it 'cos it caught the sun. Easy to miss. My guess, whoever dumped it wouldn't have planned on it hooking on a tree. No one would've found it if it dropped to the valley. Too rugged down there. I reckon from the weed growth begun in that dint that it's a month at most. We've had a sprinkle of rain in the last while. Be enough to germinate them.'

Avery nodded, made a move towards the battered fridge.

'I broke the lock. Sorry. Had no idea what I was gonna find. Brace yourself.'

Then Cal felt silly saying that last comment. As if Avery wouldn't have had countless gruesome scenes to work in his time.

Hassett followed Avery. They'd both gloved up. Avery took the pry-bar from where Cal had dropped it and used the tip to lever between the edge of the seals where there were less likely to be prints. He opened the lid. Hassett covered his mouth as the vault released its putrid reek. Avery stoic, taking in the contents before dropping the lid.

'You mind if we hang onto this for now? Techs will want to verify the tool-marks.' He held Cal's pry-bar.

'No probs. How 'bout my straps?' She indicated the webbing ribbons still attached to the winch hook.

Avery sucked air through his teeth. 'They'll want them too I imagine. Sorry. You got any more?' Avery aware of the critical need for such equipment out in the bush.

Cal had a second, worn and partially frayed pair onboard. She gave a glum assent.

'Get on your way if you like. There'll be follow-up at some point,' Avery finished.

'All good.'

Cal walked to the cab of her truck, started it and slowly drove off, leaving the officers with her grisly find.

She drove along the ridge for nearly an hour. Throughout her journey she couldn't stop thinking of the freezer and its contents. If it turned out those contents were human remains, that was the second time in less than three months she'd come across such a tragic discovery. Is this what you signed up for Nyx, she wondered. It always brought her up short, the brutality that befell some people, the savagery some human animals were capable of. Rocks pummeled the underside of the truck. She flicked her eyes to her rear-view mirror where a rolling plume of dust exited from beneath the vehicle like a yellow mist hovering over the lonely track.

Finally she slowed and stopped at a side-track on the edge of the road. The entrance was blocked by a heavy galvanized pipe gate, hung on an eight-inch diameter galv post concreted into the ground. A beefy padlock was shrouded in a quarter-inch steel-plate protector that prevented cutting of the shackle. Cal used her key, one of only half a dozen in existence. She drove through and re-locked the gate then looked up into the trees on either side of the track. Remote operated, solar-powered cameras mounted in the branches with motion sensors.

The Jurassic survivors were precious. From a natural resource point-of-view they were priceless; a singular, spectacular relic of a long-ago millennia. Their rarity as a unique species meant they also had value to collectors around the globe. Some who had no respect for protecting the specimens in their wild habitat. Like those who sought and exploited threatened animal species, there were individuals who created demand for endangered plant species as well. Their already precarious survival further pressured. Cal felt a profound sense of duty in her role as protector.

If someone were to look on a map for the secret valley where the Mallami ferns grew they would never have considered a track that diverged from the right-hand side of the ridge. It fell away to the river-flats of the Hawkesbury in the northeast. Unknown to most, twelve k's down the mountain trail, Cal traversed a saddle track on a lower, secondary ridge that skirred off around the edge of the main range. It worked its way back to the west and the endless valley tracts inland. It was rugged, narrow and hidden from above by rock overhangs and tenacious scrub. The topography alone restricted access but, still, no amount of care or stealth was misplaced.

Her ranger wagon bumped and bounced as she made her deliberate progress along the craggy path. She yawned and realized she'd missed her usual mid-morning coffee and she was hungry as well. The find on the ridge-top had stymied any appetite but she couldn't afford any lapse of attention on this drive. She drew in a deep breath and went to knock the air-con up a notch to sharpen herself. *Nope. Already done that. Wakey wakey Nyx.* She roughed her cheek and forehead with one hand, visualized the pathway ahead and knew she could take a break in about five k's. She stretched her neck and drove on.

When she reached her rest-stop, a trackside culvert where a waterfall ran during the wet-season, she got out and lifted the side-window panel of the rear deck cover. She pulled out a tiny burner and coffee pot and set them going. She'd made herself a sandwich that morning but couldn't face the idea of eating. She remembered the malodorous reek earlier that day. Her stomach made an involuntary convulsion. She waited for her espresso. If her hunger returned later and eventually overrode her nausea, she had tinned food supplies. Like most bush travellers, she carried plenty of water, food and fuel.

She was in the shade but it was still sticky and humid. She could hear lizards and skinks scrabbling along the rock above her where the sun hit and baked the cliff-face.

Her coffee pot hissed and she poured the brew, went to the front of her truck and leaned on the bumper as she drank and pondered her morning. The vast and often unpopulated stretches of the hinterland seemed to have a number of effects on the more recent inhabitants of this land. Many seemed to view the endless reaches of forest, scrubland or desert as a terrifying and confronting emptiness. Others assessed this apparent vacuum as an ideal hidey-hole for their misdeeds, exploiting the fears of their countrymen to keep their transgressions undiscovered. As someone who valued the quiet and isolation of the rich surrounds Cal was more likely than most to trip upon an errant dumping. Where would this latest find lead?

Later that day, her sometime squeeze DI Liz Scobie would no doubt be briefed and an inquiry would kick-off. For now, Cal had her own pressing job. Checking the status of the Mallami ferns in the secret valley.

***

Back on The Lyrebird Track Avery briefed the forensic techs and left them to their work. When they were done at the scene the freezer would be plastic wrapped and lifted into a trailer before the contents were transported to the lab for testing. He made a quick call on the sat-phone to his boss, DI Liz Scobie at Richmond Command, down below the mountains.

'Looks like human remains. Techs are doing their thing. Might need a crew on this. Pathologist says young female at this stage. I'll fill you in later. Be a while here still.'

'Thanks Glen. I can get them going here on Mispers. If you miss me tonight we'll catch-up first thing.'

'Gotcha Skip.'

Chapter 3

THE GOAT TRACK FLATTENED out into the ancient river valley, carved over millennia through the sandstone. The way was still rugged but at least she didn't have to negotiate avoiding a five hundred metre drop over a cliff edge. She drove another ten ks through the scrub and parked her truck beneath a copse of saplings to obscure it from above. Subterfuge wasn't a primary tactic in her work, but the Mallemi's were precious and called for heightened vigilance. As did out-of-season hunters and poachers. The last part of her trek would be made on foot. Gathering her measuring equipment and sample boxes, she re-checked her pack, locked the truck and set off.

Heavy charcoal coloured clouds sat low on the horizon to the south, obliterating the light as a storm-front moved up the Hawkesbury from the coast. She'd need to be quick to beat it. No tent sleeping tonight. The rear canopy of the truck would be drier and cosier when that lot dumped their deluge.

She strode into the scrub, the ground around her arid rubble. As she neared the narrow canyon and turned into the shadows of the sheer walls the atmosphere changed immediately. She could smell the moisture and decay of the fern fronds, a bitter tang. The rock faces shut-off the north and western heat and light. Any water that travelled here, both underground and via the cliffs when it rained, was held and protected by the cool rock walls and the overstorey vegetation. Even the moisture exhaled by the transpiring fronds was maintained and recycled in a tiny and specific micro-climate, protected by the tree canopy above.

She dropped her pack and began her tasks quickly, in preference to a more methodical pace where she could consider her finds as she worked. It just wasn't a day for that with the storm-front approaching beyond the clifftops. She noted measurements in her log, took samples and photographs, glancing upwards to the sky at the canyon entrance every few minutes. Canyons were dangerous places in flash floods with nowhere to escape.

She continued with her rapid note-taking until her focus was broken by the crackle and boom of the squall. The air smelt distinctly of metallic charge like bleach and burnt plastic.

Thrusting her gear into her rucksack she checked herself from breaking into a run. Undue speed through that landscape was dangerous. As she cleared out of the sandstone walls into open ground the rain hit like a cosmic waterfall, drenching and stinging her exposed skin as she navigated the rock-strewn ground in front of her. Still several hundred metres from her truck she gave up on staying dry or protecting herself. Water coursed from her head and forearms as she gripped her pack-straps.

A thick charge of lightning lit the dim surrounds and blasted the nearby cliff wall with white light. A huff of shock escaped her throat. The attendant thunder boom only made her fright worse. Just get to the truck, get inside she cajoled herself.

She threw her body across the driver's seat and pulled the door behind her. Her hair and clothes seeped water as she drew her body away from anything metallic inside the cab. She closed her eyes as the barrage of noise and alternating light pelted and blared around her.

After the worst of the squall had passed, Cal released herself from the cab and climbed into the back of the truck under the plastic canopy. She changed out of her wet clothes, unfurled her bedroll and stretched out.

As she stared into the darkness, the land around her settled. Water filtered through the rocks and soil. Creatures wandered and fed. The early images from her day reformed and, as she shook them away, all that remained was an endless scroll of women's and girl's names, receding in time.

Chapter 4

Next morning at Richmond Command Scobie went towards her office, passing DS Glen Avery's desk.

'Morning Glen. Give me five then come to my office. We'll update.'

Avery leaned back in his chair, raised his arms in a stretch, yawned.

'Morning Skip. Will do.'

He gave Scobie time to put her things in order and drink half her coffee before he sauntered over with his notebook and laptop. He gave a light rap on the door-jamb and entered.

Scobie was seated. She palmed the hair at the side of her head, though nothing was out of place.

'Ruddy had a cursory on Mispers last night,' referring to junior officer, Constable Claudia Rudnick. Resting her fingers on a list, 'Did she email a copy to you?'

'Yup. I'm waiting on pathology to see if we can narrow our focus. Nothing more for you since last night except to say it appears the freezer had been buried, possibly for some time. Bit of an odd one really. Why remove something that's safely hidden? Unless it was potentially about to be unearthed and the perp knew and had to move swiftly.'

'Like impending earthworks on a building site?'

Avery shrugged.

'Maybe. Still, risky. If techs can give us something from soil analysis we can get a range and tailor it for Mispers. Still, don't reckon someone would go far beyond their local area carrying something like that. Even if it is the middle-of-nowhere out there.'

'I've given you Ruddy and you've got Gav. When we know more we'll reassess personnel. Thanks Glen.'

Avery slapped his notebook against his thigh and nodded as he turned and left her office.

'All good,' he said.

***

Cal woke early the morning after the storm. Her first thought: the find in the freezer on the Lyrebird Track. A pall of sadness came over her. *Maybe it was just old meat. Then why the human skull? And why that hellish rubber mask?* She felt queasy almost immediately. Wondered if Scobie and her crew had any news.

At least she'd managed to get her fern data before the squall hit yesterday. She made coffee and checked her phone but was too close to the cliffs to get reception and her sat-phone wasn't called for. She considered eating a protein bar as she breathed in the crisp air. A bright, pale sky overhead. She'd not eaten in twenty-four hours. But the idea still nauseated her.

The surrounds always seemed clean and fresh after a storm, debris notwithstanding. She checked everything was properly stowed in her tool lockers on the rear deck then fired up her truck and left the Valley. She ascended the lumpy rock trail at a cautious crawl with tyres jumping and grinding over the hacked and blasted surface.

Back up near the apex of the ridge she passed through the narrow entryway and locked the gate. She checked for approaching vehicles but, as per every visit, nothing else was around. Still, she didn't like to be seen at the gateway and didn't want to linger. She quickly looked up to where she knew the remote cameras were and confirmed they were intact visually. The air smelt bright and sharp as if the lightning had seared all the impurities from the atmosphere. She was certain she'd have clearing work to do where the storm had passed above the valley floor back near Three Rivers. Sure enough, her Spot X sat-messenger pinged as she re-checked the gate padlock. One from her boss, Fisho.

-Report of trees down on the Lower Three Rivers Track. Can you check and clear? Assuming you survived the night.

Another text, this one from Scobie.

-When you get a moment, let me know you're OK x

Cal flicked off a quick reply to Scobie then fired an affirmative to her boss. Having clear air overhead meant the sat-device worked well. And it didn't need tethering to her mobile. Another plus. Some of the environments and activities she plied weren't easy on vulnerable glass and plastic.

The top track was littered with leaves and twigs after the big blow, the dust captured by the rain squall and trapped until the heat desiccated it into airborne grit again. She drove back along the ridge, eventually passing the police tape marking the site she'd found the previous day. She was keen to hear if Scobie had any update on that matter.

Down through the forest Cal wound along the overhung valley track, following the old stream trail. Her wheels crushed small branches and deadfall that had cracked off when the winds had blasted through. She drove half-expecting a downed tree across the road at any moment.

But what she did come across was a vehicle listing awkwardly at the roadside edge.

Chapter 5

Cal pulled in ahead of the stranded vehicle, tucking her truck as safely as she could on the mushy margins.

A guy was lying beside the rear corner panel of a blue Mitsubishi sedan. His leg was trapped under the door sill and it appeared that the vehicle had fallen off its jack in the soft soil. The bare wheel hub was mashed into the dirt where it had dropped and the removed wheel was lying flat on the banked earth behind the car. The ground declined at a steep angle beyond the road edge.

The man had both hands clamped around his thigh as though he was trying to squeeze the pain away. The upper part of his body rocked back and forth and he groaned in a low, pained anguish. Cal wondered if his lower leg might be fractured. Leg breaks, rural accidents. Comes with the territory she surmised as she approached, steeling herself.

'Get you some help mate.'

She put a hand on his shoulder. He opened his eyes briefly then closed them again. She checked she had signal on her phone and considered making a call to the local volunteer fire brigade to help lift the vehicle. Then decided she could manage with her own jack. But she'd still have to wait for a doctor or paramedic. As soon as the blood flowed beyond that visible constriction, well, it didn't bear thinking about. The nearest doctor's surgery was in Warriga Flat.

Cal stood away from the injured guy as she rang and spoke to the receptionist at the small medical centre.

'I can't see a lot of blood but there may well be a fracture. I don't wanna lift the vehicle before the doc arrives. Should I do anything meantime?'

'No food or drink. Keep them warm. Don't move them unless they're in danger. Otherwise, just wait for the doctor. He'll be there in about twenty minutes.'

'They'll bring pain-killers, yeh?'

'Yes. I'm ringing for an ambulance from Clarendon. The doctor can help until they get there.'

Cal went to her work-truck, grabbed her jacket and a thermal blanket from the rear of the cab and took them over to the guy who was groaning on the ground. Well, no need to worry about the "don't move them" scenario she thought. The guy was utterly pinned to the earth.

'Doc's on his way mate. If you'd be more comfortable lying back, I can put this under your head. Just don't move anything lower down.'

She showed her rolled jacket. The guy nodded as she gently slipped it under his head. He leaned back, hands still clamped to his thigh.

'Just gonna try and keep you warm,' as she flapped open the thermal blanket, 'Won't move you. Just gonna tuck it around you, okay?'

The guy squeezed his eyes shut and nodded slightly. Cal eased the foil cloth around the exposed parts of his torso using her fingers to push it in under his body, cocooning him to trap the heat. Being morning in the valley, and with the damp after the storm, it wasn't as warm as it could have been. Probably a different story up on top of the exposed ridges. Cal finished tucking the thermal around his shoulders and held her arm there.

'Flats are a bloody nuisance, ay. Jeez, some of my outback trips, felt like I was doing a tyre change on the hour. Must be the heat as well as the state of those tracks, just blows them out,' she jabbered on, trying to keep him distracted.

'What's your name mate? I'm Cal.'

'Nathan,' he croaked.

'You a local? Day-tripper?'

The guy continued to rock in small movements as if to convince himself of his agency even though his leg was trapped.

'Too much to talk? Okay, I'll just waffle on then. How 'bout some Latin plant names? I'll make it tricky. These ones are from across the ditch in NZ. That's my homeland if you didn't catch the accent. I'll say the name, you guess the plant. Okay, let's start with *Melicytis ramiflorus*. Ring any bells?'

Nathan's eyes were clenched tightly. Cal reached for his shoulder, gave a squeeze.

'You're gonna be okay mate. Help's on the way. Just stay with me.'

Cal looked skyward, but the bush and rock overhangs obliterated everything.

'Okay, you struck out of the first one. Let's see how you go with number two. *Bracyglottis repanda*. I'll give you a little hint. We call it bush toilet-paper in NZ. No?'

'Fuuuuck,' Nathan moaned, 'I can't fuckin stand it.'

He grimaced and tried to swing himself upwards like he could get away from the pain.

'Steady fella. You're doing real good. I know it doesn't feel like it. Help's coming. Gimme your hand. C'mon, squeeze. Squeeze my fist. That's it, hard as you can. Wanna punch me? For the stupid plant names? C'mon, throw one. Open your eyes, hit my hand,' she held it open like you would a practice mitt, 'Punch me.'

All she got was a guttural moan.

'Do it Nathan. Hit me or I'll go back to the plant names. They'll be here soon. Let's try some local species.'

The time stretched and Cal rabbited on with as much nonsense as she could conjure and gave what she hoped were soothing assurances to the distressed guy.

Finally, Cal could hear a vehicle engine and the rattle of gravel bouncing from the underbody as it neared them. A sleek, dark blue BMW SUV rounded the bend beyond. Cal hoped it was the doctor. The driver pulled in just ahead of the stranded Mitsubishi. He got out, went to the rear of the SUV and returned carrying a medical holdall. His build was trim and he was very tall, maybe two metres. He wore a cream linen shirt with navy-blue trousers and he moved with a quiet efficiency as he crouched beside the injured man and Cal.

'Good to see you,' Cal raised an eyebrow, 'This is Nathan.'

'Hugh Pinder,' the doctor said as he looked over the prone guy. He put his fingers to Nathan's wrist, stared into his eyes.

'You with me Nathan?'

The injured guy winced and gave a small nod. Pinder glanced at the leg and the swelling above the constriction.

'Ambos are on their way Nathan. We'll get you sorted.'

Pinder gently examined Nathan's leg above where it was stuck under the car. He turned to Cal.

'Would be good if we could access the wound and get a sterile bandage on it. Have you looked underneath the vehicle?'

'There's no room to get under with the car sitting on this bank. And the ground here is too unstable to jack it. I think we need to wait for more hands.'

Pinder nodded.

'Okay Nathan. I'm just going to give you some pain relief.'

It was another ten minutes before they heard the approaching ambulance. Cal stood back while the two paramedics assessed the situation and spoke with Pinder.

Then one of the paramedics came and spoke with her.

'We need to lift that vehicle. If we can't do it, we'll need to call the firies from Three Waters. Do you have any lifting gear in your truck?'

Cal considered a moment.

'I've got a jack and a come-along,' she paused and looked around, above the medical scene, 'I've got a recovery winch on the truck. Just wondering if I could hook it over a tree limb. There's nothing above the car there. But down the bank there's some big angophoras. I could climb one of those tall ones and throw the hook over a solid branch. Should be higher than the road here. I can use that high limb as a pulley. Lift the car long enough for you to pull him out safely. Whaddaya reckon? You guys can do traffic control while I set up.'

'Sounds like a plan.'

The paramedic moved smartly over to the others and relayed the idea while Cal ran to her truck and manoeuvred it on the roadway to the front of the stranded car. She kept her engine running and ran the winch cable out before scrambling down the bank to a eucalypt with a branch of decent girth and height to give her a lifting point. She clamped the winch cable and hook around her waist and began ascending the trunk. Her boots weren't the best for the task, sliding on the surface of the bark, but she used her arms to keep pulling herself up until she was nearly six metres aloft.

She kicked at the bough she'd selected to test its integrity and satisfied that it was sound, she unhooked the cable and threw it around the heavy branch, dropping the hook back down to the ground. The lift point wasn't that much higher than the car but it would direct the pull upwards enough. She hoped.

Cal shimmied down the trunk, burning her forearms as she quickly descended. The other ambo had come down the bank and carried the cable and hook-end back up to the roadside. They all waited on Cal.

She climbed the bank and crawled under the car with the hook attachment to where there was a tight gap beside the remaining intact rear wheel. She looked for a lifting point. The rear mounting of the suspension was ideal, but it was barely above the ground. She crawled as close as she could and stretched her hand behind the mount to loop the hook over and back around on itself. The hook wouldn't fit through the gap. She had so little room to move. She tried again, her arm aching from supporting the heavy hook and cable. This time she jammed the hook side on and tried to push from behind it. Finally, the thing slipped through the gap. Cal quickly thumbed open the spring clamp on the hook and sent the cable behind locking it in. She wriggled out from under the car keeping the rest of the cable in her hand, routing it so it wouldn't snag. Pinder and the other paramedic were crouched beside Nathan. The other was waiting by Cal's truck.

'All good?' the ambo asked.

'Sweet. I hope.' She flipped the lever on the winch and took up the slack in the cable.

'Okay. I'm gonna lift slow and steady.'

She paused for the ambo to suggest the best procedure from their point of view.

'The three of us will work fast to board-splint that break and drag him out. Guess you've gotta hold that car free meantime.'

'I can lock this and come help. But we have to be quick.'

'Nah. Too risky. You stay with the winch. Let's do it.'

Once the medics were in position around Nathan with the splint boards and stretcher they gave Cal a nod.

She hit the winch lever. The electric motor whirred and the wire cable began to wind around the spool. Cal watched the back of the car as the wire pulled taut running around the wheel-arch and up the side panel. The wire bit into the paintwork and stretched across the rear of the car then bridged across the incline and dug into the bark of the bough. The tree branch bent slightly as it took the strain. The back corner of the car moved incrementally across towards the trees as it lifted. Nathan let out a gasp that Cal could hear over the whine of the electric motor. She kept watching, scanning, from the car to the tree to the medical helpers. The car body was lifting. The wire crumpled the thin panel as more weight went through it. There was a gap of about 150mm now where the car body had fallen on Nathan. The ambos were edging the splint boards alongside the leg. Cal checked the tree bough. It looked stable. Still the car rear rose. The opposite wheel digging into the ground as the car body rolled towards that side.

'All good there?' Cal called over to the others.

'Nearly there. Need maybe another ten centimetres. Can you do it?' Pinder called back as the other two worked at aligning the splint before moving Nathan out.

Cal looked towards the tree. She could see naked wood where the cable had torn the bark down to the new growth. The loop had slid a few centimetres along the tapering branch. If it slipped much further it could slide right off.

'Okay. Be quick you guys.'

Cal eased the winch lever. Her eyes flicked from the bough to the car. The paramedics were securing the leg splint as they crouched in the tight space. Cal looked back to the tree.

Please hold, she begged silently to the universe.

Back to the car. Now the three were dragging Nathan out from under, Pinder and one paramedic dragging from his shoulders, the other ambo stabilising his leg.

Cmon. Cal gritted her teeth. *Get him outa there.*

She looked back towards the tree bough just as the cable slid under the bark, sliding away from the thickest part closest to the trunk. Cal heard the creak and the judder as the car dropped. She swung her head back to the car as it swayed and tipped, still above ground, Nathan removed to safety. Cal looked back at the tree where a node of wood from an old fallen branch wound was holding the cable, for now.

'I gotta drop it.' She called. 'Stand clear.'

When she saw they were out of the way, she set the winch in reverse and released the tension on the cable, slowly setting the car down. When it hit ground, she ran over to help carry Nathan's stretchered body into the ambulance.

Pinder returned his gear to the BMW and addressed Cal as he climbed in the driver's door.

'Job done.'

'Many hands and all that. See ya 'round.'

Cal retrieved her winch gear then dragged the stranded Mitsubishi further along the road using her tow strap.

On stable ground she replaced the flat tyre with the spare wheel. At least the vehicle could be safely towed now. She figured the owner wouldn't be driving for a while if his leg was in a cast. Now, what to do with the car keys? Cops might want to move it elsewhere. There was a small single cop station in Wirriga Flat. Richmond Police had overseen the body find up on the Lyrebird Ridge because detectives were required, plus the site there was closer to the larger centre anyway. Might be best if she just hung onto the keys. She called the Wirriga station and explained the situation in a voice message.

The injured guy scenario had completely distracted her. Now that was dealt with the freezer returned with a vengeance. She sensed her find was something dark, not banal. She craved further insight. But she was stuck on a valley floor with scratchy phone coverage. She needed to carry on with her workday, heading further along the Lower Three Rivers Track, clearing storm damage.

Chapter 6

Cal stopped twice within the next two kilometres to clear the road. The first blockage was branches and storm debris that, though numerous, didn't require power equipment to clear. She just dragged and raked debris off the roadway.

The second stop took more effort. A dead tree had blown over and downed several saplings from the high side of the road. A narrow tunnel remained beside the bank and the few cars that may have passed that way earlier in the morning had squeezed under judging by the tyre tracks through the crushed leaf debris. Must've been one of those driver's who'd alerted her boss of the obstruction. It wasn't a full road-block, but it was dangerous and needed clearing. This time she had to fire up the chainsaw. She worked methodically and had the way cleared in less than an hour. She packed her gear and carried on along the Lower Three Rivers Track.

Fifteen minutes later she approached the clearing where an early settlers' cemetery was sited. She pulled into a small parking strip, a lay-by on the side of the road that edged one of the numerous tributaries feeding the

Hawkesbury River. The surrounds were shaded by the forest that grew on both sides of the steep gully walls and the stream's path had cut deeply down through the sandstone walls over millennia. The only sunlight that penetrated directly onto the area was in the mid to late afternoon when the sun's rays pierced through a valley between two ranges beyond the Hawkesbury several ks to the west.

Inside the low fenced area a historic cemetery site bordered by the stream was crisscrossed with tree-trunks, dark and decayed or smashed and tangled among sturdier upright specimens. It was a chaotic mess overlaying the recent work done by volunteers.

A local group had been weeding and clearing graves, holding back the obliteration by encroaching bush and flooding stream. There were far fewer locals now. Many had long moved on to bigger towns looking for work and better prospects. But relatives of those buried returned for occasional weekend working bees to help maintain old family graves. The most recent session had opened the area up and revealed the breadth of the small cemetery until the previous day's storm had brought down several trees.

The small parking area had a simple, low wooden pole barrier and recently a vehicle had nudged into the fence and dislodged a horizontal shaft from its post. Cal checked it more closely. It was something she could repair then and there. Before she began she stepped over the barrier to view the recent volunteer efforts.

Quite impressive. Last time she'd visited the cemetery it was fast disappearing under Mother Nature's cycle of reclamation. The relentless edict to fill a vacuum, cover bare ground to protect its fecundity.

Cal could understand the reverence and need to pay homage people felt towards their sacred areas. She thought too of other burial sites, even older, both in her homeland and where she currently lived. Places previously disregarded and bulldozed for roads and developments, not extended the same respect or significance. The cynic in her noted how hard it was to connect to the history if the sites weren't protected.

The fallen trees from the storm were something she could clear on her own. Nothing too big or dangerously hung-up, but still: the unpredicability of rotten wood always required caution. First job was to fix the carpark fence rail.

Back at her truck she unloaded her equipment from one of the rear deck lockers. As she reached in for a heavy club-hammer and cordless driver drill her phone rang. Scobie.

All she could make out was metallic gurgling like the signal was fighting its way up from a trough in the Pacific Ocean. Cal looked skywards, not that much of it was visible. She was in a tight river valley surrounded by steep sandstone cliffs and rainforest. She thumbed a text that might send when the signal improved.

-Stuck in a valley DI. Will try and call when I get on a ridge x

As she sent the text another arrived from Scobie.

-Freezer was moved. Been buried. Young female.

Cal blew an exclamation through her teeth. Why unbury a tomb? She parked the idea momentarily to focus on her work. It wasn't easy.

She unscrewed the damaged metal hasp on the fence and beat it back into shape using the hammer on a curve of the pole. What else had Scobie's techs discovered?

She went back to the truck and got some larger gauge screws then hefted the horizontal pole back into alignment, put the metal hasp into place and screwed it in. Sorted.

With her chainsaw and safety gear in hand she began to deal with the downed trees. Most of the fallen debris ranged from rotten to rock-dry hardwood. She pulled her small file and did a quick pass over the teeth then checked the fuel and chain-oil levels. She was supposed to wear a full face-shield and helmet but hated the gear because it fogged up. In her book vision overrode the problematic safety gear when downing trees. Kinda reminiscent of the rifle she had hidden in a plastic tube attached underneath her vehicle. Not kosher ranger equipment but she wouldn't travel her rounds without it. She dragged on her protective chaps. She was on her own and a gashed leg could be fatal. Overcoming her gung-ho tendencies required constant internal nagging.

She slipped her hands into leather gloves, dropped ear-protectors into place and began chopping splintered trunks and branches into manageable pieces. When she was done cutting she tossed the chunks into the scrub bordering the gravesites where they could safely decompose.

As a ranger, she did minimal work on the cemetery site for public safety reasons. But alone she couldn't maintain the area with all her other routine requirements in the vast reserves. The volunteer working bees gave her a real boost, the endeavours of others matching her solitary efforts. Many gravestones and wooden markers were now visible where they hadn't been previously. Several of the gravesites were delineated by a type of ironwork fretwork, similar to the fences and verandas on old, terraced houses in Sydney.

By mid-afternoon the sun shone across the site via a gap in the western escarpment. Cal was hot and tired. Fatigue and chainsaws: not a happy mix. Time for a break she chivvied herself. She grabbed her water bottle then stood and stretched before wandering among the cleared graves, some she'd not seen before. Cal read the headstones in the still, heavy air. So many young deaths she thought with a hint of melancholy. *Tough times*. Some of the names were repeated and familiar in the existing community. Others strange and unheard of by her, as if genealogical lines had ended centuries ago, never to return. Chubbet, Twible, Pescud.

All kinds of British names. Celtic? Did other Europeans settle there she wondered? Walking further towards a shaded area on the edge of the cemetery she came across a broken headstone, the fallen top repositioned and propped from behind with large rocks. Isa Braam, she read. That one didn't sound English.

'I hope you don't mind me joining you today Isa. I usually sit yonder on the other side with Jacob but he's still covered with fallen trees and I haven't cleared him yet.'

She unscrewed her water bottle and drank the lot. With the sun behind her she listened for a few moments to the peaceful murmurings of the graveyard.

She returned her gear to the truck, weary as she reloaded. Gazing up to the top of the distant range where she'd been the previous day, she wondered if someone local had dumped that grim freezer with the human skull inside? She'd been too distressed to inspect the contents further. Were those the remains of a complete body in there? Encased inside an old domestic freezer. That idea was somehow more poignant than the shocking death itself. That it had also been buried, dug up and finally tossed over a cliff pointed to someone not forgetting. And that someone was likely the person who put the body inside in the first place.

The long passage of time seemed to underline the neglect, the forgotten individual invisibilised over time. Perhaps that wasn't the case at all. Maybe a family somewhere still wondered every day where their missing relative was. Or, what if that character had no relatives, no one to wonder and hope? She was keen to know what Scobie and her team had come up with.

She locked down her toolboxes and climbed into the cab then headed back along the river flats, south to Kurrajong.

Chapter 7

Cal arrived at her Kurrajong cabin and parked at the shady rear. It was a converted shearers' quarters on the property of a friend, Dee, a local vet. Cal had two bolt-holes; one there in the Hawkesbury region close to the National Parks where she worked and another in Petersham in Sydney's Inner West. Cal pictured the sleepout behind her Aunt Zinnia's cottage where she'd stayed when she was younger or when visiting mates in town. But Zin had recently passed away and Cal was still figuring out what to do with the Petersham cottage. She still felt a raw grief at Zinnia's passing. There was a newer sadness that her aunt had never met Spike, a young homeless local currently living in Petersham with Dif, Cal's foster brother.

Having been away from Kurrajong for a few days she went straight to her mini fernery and checked the misting system. She was determined to nurse along the fernlings she'd been tasked with raising, trialing various climatic conditions and growing mediums to find the optimum range. The lean-to was on the leeside of her cabin with a combination of shade-cloth and clear corrugated polycarb to provide enough light and air without losing the required humidity. It wasn't strictly part of her job but Cal was part of the small group looking after them in the wild. She and two others raised the ferns in separate areas to try and ensure their continued survival as the entire region was prone to bushfires. It was often a heart-breaking experiment, but she was one of several parks' staff, amateur enthusiasts and scientists who were each doing their bit to build up stocks of the unique and ancient ferns.

She'd installed a tank to catch roof-water and a small twelve-volt solar-powered pump to feed the misters with a back-up from the main supply. All seemed okay.

Her phone rang. Scobie. Finally they could speak to each other.

'How's tricks DI?'

'Been worried about you. You obviously survived the storm. How are you feeling after your find on the Lyrebird? You okay hon?'

'Yeh. I've been a bit disturbed I guess. Do you know anything yet?'

'You know you can get some counseling after what happened.'

'I'm fine Scobes. What news from yonder freezer?'

'It's taking them a while to sift through. The skeleton suggests a female, probably under thirty. Bones are yet to be X-rayed, no obvious damage to the skull. Very little else, as you can imagine. Those remains have been there a long time. They're hoping they'll find something in the liquid or the structure. I'm not holding my breath.'

'Mmm. Weird one.'

'It is. And hard to pin a time frame on it to get a start on Mispers. We could be going back decades. We just have be patient. How was your fern-check jaunt?'

'Not on a holiday Scobes. It is my work y'know.'

'You love the rough escapades, don't lie.'

Cal hitched her chin in a silent scoff but couldn't argue.

'Ferns are holding their own for now and that's always a relief. Might be a different story in a month or so, way the temps are up already. I'm heading into Petersham tonight. Wanna get together later?'

'I'd like that very much.'

She heard him before she saw him. The arhythmic patter of her tripod buddy, Banjo, Dee's red-heeler rescue. Cal turned in a half-crouch before he had a chance to boof his head into the back of her knee. Scary arms out ready to grab him. He barked, tipping back onto his hind legs as she buried her fingers into the coarse ruff at his neck.

'C'mon my lovely.'

She grabbed her overnight bag and haversack from the cab and headed indoors.

Banjo's mangled rubber toy bounced at her feet as she struggled through the doorway.

'Tryin'o kill me bro?'

Cal turned and booted the thing beyond the veranda. Banjo followed.

She dumped her bags, filled her espresso pot and answered an incoming call from Dif.

'How's your timing mate.' She spoke.

'Sublime and nuanced.'

'Unlike your hair-style. Just back from the whoop-whoops.'

'I figured. You coming into town?'

'Booty call with Scobie. Not to be missed.'

'TMI. Hey, be good to catch-up. Where's my angle grinder.'

'Aw. Sorry mate. Burnt it out. Meant to replace it before you noticed. Can you wait?'

'Guess I'll have to won't I.'

'How's Junior?' Cal grabbed a small mug from an open shelf.

'Spike's all good. Running out of projects to keep them occupied though. Pretty fast learner. I think we might need to compile a list. A long one.'

'I hear ya. If I don't see ya tonight, how 'bout brunch tomoz?'

'Sweet.'

Cal filled the washing machine, drank her coffee while entertaining Banjo from the deck, then showered and threw a change of clothes into her carryall. She dressed in scuffed biker boots, clean faded denims, a cap-sleeved black t-shirt and a plaid black and blue woolen jacket cut in a classic western style. Her version of 'going to trouble' for Scobie.

Still without a road-worthy replacement for her old Ford. The painful image of the burnt-out carcass on the South Coast almost made her weep. She left in her work truck heading for Sydney.

Chapter 8

CAL LEFT PETERSHAM AND she drove straight to the nearest mega hardware store. She grabbed a heavy duty 100mm angle grinder to replace the one of Dif's she'd trashed. Instead of going through the check-out, she went to the help desk and asked the staffer to gift-wrap it.

'And a bow if you have one,' Cal winked.

She stashed the parcel behind her seat and carried on to Scobie's place in Alexandria.

Cal parked in the back lane at the rear of Scobie's apartment. Got buzzed through the security gate. As she raced up the stairs she could smell the waft of fenugreek and cumin. Another of Scobie's famous curries she thought.

Scobie held the door open. She'd changed out of her work gear and showered. She now wore jeans and a floaty, suggestive number that clung in all the right places. Her damp hair was pulled up in a casual knot.

Cal slipped an arm around her waist, kissed her.

'Get you something to drink?' Scobie walked through to the kitchen.

'Water's good.'

'You eaten?'

'Uh uh.'

'Cooking if you're hungry.' Scobie passed her a tall glass of chilled water, a lemon wedge on the rim.

'Aw. Spoiling me again. Smells good. How'd you go today? Any news?'

'You do know I invite you here as a distraction?' Scobie stirred the contents of a large saucepan, tapped the wooden spoon on the rim and then rested it on a saucer. She peered at Cal with one eyebrow cocked.

'Sorry. Guess I'm a bit invested in this one.'

'And the last one. And the one before that.' Scobie rinsed fresh coriander at the sink. Shook the water off and began chopping it on a board.

'Hey, I work in the low-life's favourite dumping ground. What can I say?'

'Okay, I'll fill you in. Then the subject is closed, for now.'

'Fair enough.' Cal held up her hands in surrender.

Scobie rinsed off the knife, wiped her hands on a towel.

'I'm having a wine. Can I get you a beer?'

'Can I grab your ass?'

'For god's sake Cal.'

'Well, if you could see what I see.'

Cal squeezed the juice from the lemon wedge into the remaining water and drained it.

Scobie rolled her eyes, took a bottle from the fridge and poured herself a glass of fruity rosé. She held up a Peroni to Cal before she closed the fridge door. Cal lifted her chin.

Scobie passed the beer to Cal and spoke quietly.

'X-rays show an old, healed fracture on her left tibia. No other obvious breaks except the hyoid bone, which, as you no doubt already know means ...'

'Probable strangulation.'

'Right. Other physical evidence from the freezer which may be useful is that the electrical plug had been swapped to a piggy-back. Snipped off and replaced. And inside the plastic liner of the freezer two letters were scratched on the bottom.'

'Oh. That's a bit odd. On the inside?'

'Yes. Weird, I agree.' Scobie rested her hip against the bench.

'Like, someone's initials maybe?'

'Maybe.'

'And the cord being cut, the plug replaced. If you could find the original, maybe match the cuts?'

'Very long-shot because we think this is possibly decades old. But theoretically, yes. Serial numbers were being followed up this arvy with the manufacturer. Other than that, fingerprints unlikely. Hair stuck inside the mask might yield something.'

'Yeh, the mask. Surprised the rubber was intact.'

Scobie sipped her wine.

'Sunlight's the worst element for deterioration of rubber. It was protected from that. I'm expecting more detail tomorrow. I understand why you're interested and you know I'll keep you in the loop. But please keep everything under your hat Cal. Now I have to switch off for a bit.'

'Course.'

'Let's talk about something else before we eat. Tell me about how your other household is getting on.'

'Or we could muck-up a bit.'

'Tell me about home.'

'But you're irresistible to me, I can't help it.'

'The car projects. How are Dif and Spike?'

'Why must you thwart me?'

'You usually ignore me so I'm not hindering anything.'

Cal gave in to the intractable Scobie.

Chapter 9

On Sydney's South Coast, DS Lyle Tambor sat stiffly before the Area Commander's heavy desk. Tambor was still dealing the repercussions of the troublesome freak, Dif Stangler, who'd several months prior tried to alert local police to a body being dumped in a local quarry. That had kicked off no end of problems for Tambor. Once again he was under scrutiny while Stangler, the gangling nonce, was being hailed as some heroic do-gooder. Tambor ground his knuckles into his thighs. Area Commander Keller regarded a print-out before him.

'A note was left at the Greyridge station and you were first officer on site that morning. Yet you made no report of this information,' Keller's eyes appraised Tambor.

'As I've previously stated, sir, it must've blown away. Who'd be dumb enough to shove a piece of paper under a door. Could've gone anywhere.'

'It was drizzling with rain on the morning Stangler claimed to have left the tip-off. I hardly think it would have blown anywhere. More likely to have stuck to the floor don't you think?'

Tambor was silent. He met Keller's stare with his own as an image of burning paper and curling ashes drifted across his memory.

'You seem to find this matter an irritation. In fact, I'd say you're contemptuous. Have you forgotten who pays our salaries?'

Tambor remained silent. Felt like nettles stung the underside of his thighs. Wanted out of the stifling room.

'I'd like a response Detective Sergeant. You might consider this an insignificant matter. It's not. A murder had occurred and a member of the public took the time to try and alert the authorities. That is us. We all make mistakes. We're human. However, this organisation is held to a higher standard. So, I repeat, who pays us?'

'Taxpayers, sir.' Tambor mumbled.

'That riles you, does it? That we're answerable?'

'Freak hasn't paid taxes in its life.'

'I don't like your attitude DS Tambor. Your actions, or lack of them, reflect on our entire organisation. It's embarrassing for all decent officers. The point is: we serve and we're accountable. Not the other way around. Might be worth your pondering that. And you're to attend a Diversity and Sensitivity Training.'

Dismissed, Tambor left the building. His blood steaming in his veins. Something wrong with this fuckin picture, he thought. Woke wankery. He lit a cigarette, drew hard on the filter, his lips pulled back across his teeth. Shook his head. Trans queer faggoty fuck. World's gone fuckin la-la.

Worse than this current annoyance however, Tambor was yet to figure out what Vic Lasprilla had meant when he last paid Tambor off.

"Don't look too closely," the property developer had said. If Lasprilla wasn't referring to the body dumped at the quarry, what exactly was he referring to?

Tambor needed clarification. He strode to his car, pulled the burner phone from the door pocket and texted Lasprilla for a meet.

***

Inside the Incident Room at Richmond Police, DI Liz Scobie had gathered the troops for a briefing. She'd drawn in other members of the wider squad to focus on the body in the freezer case. This included experienced detectives Janice Ottering, Len Birch and Glen Avery. Gavin Hassett and Claudia Rudnick were the juniors.

'Janice, have you come up with anything on Mispers?'

'Glen's on that, Skip.'

'Course. Sorry. Glen?'

'Though we have nothing geographically in that location we do have possibles from Central Coast, Sydney and even the South Coast. But I think it's a stretch anyone would drive with a body that far before dumping it.'

'It's been done,' Len Birch drawled.

'Unsuccessfully. Early eighties. Dipstick from Albion Park down south thought he was being clever. Got his vehicle stuck in an unfamiliar area hours away from his patch near Blaxland. Group of hunters came by and helped get him out. One was a retired cop. Recognised the smell coming from the boot. Idiot got nabbed.' Birch sucked his teeth. 'Agree with Glen though. Unlikely.'

'Still, I'd like any missing women from that time-frame, maybe five years either side. So, nineteen ninety until two-thousand, anyone whose measurements tally physically. Let's just be thorough.' Scobie scanned some paperwork on her desktop.

'So if the freezer was moved, are you thinking that too could have come from well beyond the region it was found? Like, not just potentially, the victim?' Ottering said.

'Well, until we have a better fix forensically, it's all wide open isn't it? Speaking of which, we're hoping soil analysis isn't far off. Interviews. Ruddy? Where are we at?'

'Still collating. Nothing striking from our initial canvas. Janice and I will cross-check when they're complete. Couple of outstanding people we're still trying to speak with. Small community but folks move around during their day.'

'Who's outstanding?' Scobie said somewhat brusquely.

Claudia Rudnick finger-scrolled her tablet.

'Ah, Felix Shifrin and Todd Norby.'

'You tried calling them? Don't these people have phones?'

Janice Ottering piped up.

'We have, Skip. Crap service out there lotta places. But if you can spare us today, I'd prefer a face-to-face.

One of them's the ferry operator at Wirriga Flat. Felix Shifrin. Most vehicles would use his service unless they were taking a lot of extra ks on back routes.'

'Which of course a lowlife dumping a body might be inclined to do,' Birch added.

'Okay. I'd like you three to go and clear up the outstanding interviews today.' Scobie turned to Gavin Hassett who was wiggling his fingers and studying his knuckles.

'Gav. You work with Glen on the Mispers. Unless something vital pops up we'll reconvene tomorrow morning and hopefully we'll have some more forensic reports in the mix then. And we'll keep the information about initials scratched into the plastic freezer liner under our hats for the time being. It won't be made public.'

Chapter 10

Next morning, after leaving Scobie's apartment, Cal drove to Petersham before later making her way to Kurrajong on Sydney's outskirts. The garage at her Aunt Zin's Petersham property had undergone a few changes. Dif, Cal's long-lost foster brother and singular family member, was now a regular in the house.

Cal strolled past the lean-to extension Dif had built off the garage to accommodate the car-mod activities going on inside the main workshop. The Datsun roadster project, gifted from her gearhead compadre Pirate, was underway. Dif was crouched in the rear shell of the roadster with an electric arc wand in his gloved hand. A rounded archway of four-inch tubing with support struts ran above the rear cabin of the sports car.

'Where'd you get the welding gear?' Cal asked when Dif flipped his mask.

'Gumtree.'

'Meaty fillet welds my bro.'

'Don't want you busted up when you give it too much toe.' Dif climbed out. 'Make yourself useful and get rid of the splatter.' He indicated the angle-grinder on the floor.

Cal pulled a grimace and mock-wobbled her head as she put on goggles and ear-protectors and took up the tool.

'Thought this was burnt out?'

'It was. I put new brushes in. Seems to be working okay.'

'Aw, an' I got you a new one.' She pouted.

'Won't go unused 'round here. Get on with it.'

Cal sent a sweep of orange sparks across the floor-pan as she finessed the small gobs of weld from the framework. It was a job she enjoyed because, like painting, the tidy results were instant. She went into a trance and didn't stop until she'd followed every surface of the new safety structure, removing all irregularities. When she was done she tossed her goggles and earmuffs. Dif was crouched in the open doorway to the yard smoking a rollie.

'Seen Spike today?' Cal asked.

'Saw them last night.'

'How were they?'

'Cool. Hung around out here. Took a bit of interest in my drawings for the frame. Might have another tech head in our midst.'

'Same when I was doing that undercoating. I'd be less anxious knowing Spike has some focus.'

Just months earlier she'd found the homeless youngster had broken into her aunt's empty house. She'd felt uncomfortable that the main cottage was now empty. Even when she visited she still used the sleepout in the yard through habit from her times with Aunt Zin. Didn't seem right the house went unused when so many peeps needed a roof over their heads. With Dif back on the scene after his own time sleeping rough both he and Spike now had a home and somewhere to work. It seemed a happy resolution.

'If they feel safe, it'll unfold.' Dif lifted his boot-heel and slipped his ciggy under, crushed it and returned it to a small tin, knowing Cal didn't like butts in the garden.

'You want some grub?' Cal said. 'Gonna make a sanga.'

'Yar yar.' Dif stood, dusted off his overalls, whacked his cap in his palm, followed Cal to Zin's kitchen.

Cal sliced thick slabs of ciabatta then put the board on the kitchen table with assorted dips and salad bits.

'That cheese is non-dairy,' she pooched her lips in the general direction.

'Hey, I get you probably want to forget about it all but you may be interested to hear this. That shifty cop Lyle Tambor. Scobie says he was hauled over the coals for what happened down south. Ignoring your tip-off.'

'He'll be carrying on regardless,' Dif said, humourless. 'Nothing'll stop him.'

'Bullet might.' Cal bit an olive.

'People like us don't get away with that stuff,' Dif said.

Cal chewed and considered her dead step-father. Felt the weight of the shotgun she'd snatched into her fourteen-year-old hands then pulled the trigger while her mother and sister bled out in the next room. Thought about what Tambor had done to Dif in recent months down at Greyridge. Prick like that with the power to indulge his cruel habits. Kept schtum.

'So, the sleeper project,' Dif said, referring to an under the radar vehicle that your average Joe would simply glance past. Beneath the numpty exterior and subtly lowered suspension might lurk a fully worked engine and drive-train.

'Grab your laptop. Let's look at some cheap Japper possibilities on Gumtree.'

'Car porn over lunch. Nice.'

Chapter 11

ON THE SOUTH COAST several hours from Sydney at the apex of a headland, two sedans were parked with their driver's side windows aligned. The drivers spoke through open windows.

DS Lyle Tambor addressed property developer Vic Lasprilla.

'Seems I misunderstood your last instructions, got my wires a bit crossed. I might need you to be a little more explicit. What exactly did you want me not investigating too closely? If it wasn't a body dropped into our local gravel works?'

'Lyle, my dear muffin. You misjudge my venal capabilities. I'm just a businessman and I don't know whether I should be flattered or offended by your estimation of me.'

'Look, Vic, just tell me what I was supposed to be turning a blind eye to. I don't like being in the dark, especially on matters pertaining to my own turf.'

'Nothing to worry about. All the hoo-ha at the quarry sucked the local attention away from any other nefarious antics that week. No problems, nothing to fix. Let's just park that item and move on. But, point noted Lyle, I'm to be less opaque in future.' Lasprilla gazed skywards. 'Nice little wedge of cash with your name on it coming through soon. We'll talk then. Right enough?'

'Yeh. All good.'

Lasprilla started his Beemer and drove off.

That was completely fucking unsatisfactory, Tambor thought. Prick seems to forget, I run the show around here. It's something more to do with that development at the escarpment. And I'm gonna sniff it out.

Tambor cruised further along the point and idled with the nose of his sedan facing towards the bottom of the bluff. Despite the mist descended low on the escarpment and the ocean's foreshortened and vaporised horizon, surfers plied the craggy reef drop-off to ride the swells.

Tambor wasn't interested in surfers. He viewed the camp on the far side of the estuary where the Land Rights flags hung limp and wet. A greasy smoke from a campfire listed in the windless air.

Despite his previous efforts the squatters prevailed. Tambor's night-time visits with a truck-borne water-blaster had dispersed the hobos and hippies from several nearby camps but this mob had proven largely intransigent.

Tambor pondered. Lasprilla has something going on. If I want those payments coming regular I need to be in the picture. He's not mentioned the squatter camp recently. Is he happy to have them there? Can't be good for business. Trying to sell primo coastal villas with that rubbish tip spoiling the vista. What's his game?

Has Lasprilla gotten wind of toxic seepage from the dumpsite further up the escarpment making its way down the hillside to the marshland and lagoon? And from there into the ocean. If that shite is moving downwards it'll be depositing heavy metals and unstable chemicals right through the development on its way. Open knowledge of that is gonna seriously dent his profits. And mine. Wonder how he's gonna mitigate that little scenario?

First things first though Lyle old son, he reminded himself. You've got increased scrutiny via the Stangler inquiry. He flicked his cigarette butt out the window. Fuckin freak. Time to make a trip north. Heads needed kickin.

Chapter 12

L ATER THAT AFTERNOON IN Kurrajong, Cal received a call from Scobie.

'I'm doing this because I know you'll want to hear. Probably no need to remind you but, as some imaginary covering of my backside, this call never happened.'

'Gotcha.'

'Few interesting things the pathologist has noted. Osseous discoloration. There are all sorts of competing chemical possibilities occurring in our particular scenario within the freezer. The bone stains are consistent with the metal copper. Dense concentrations of copper salts are toxic to biological agents of putrefaction. The wet environment inside the freezer would have driven the corrosion -'

'Whoa Scobes. Slow down.'

'Stay with me. Copper is unique amongst certain metals as it forms its own protective layer when corrosion occurs. But the freezer also had poor aeration which supports anaerobic bacterial activity. Which is ideal for the formation of hydrogen sulfide which occurs naturally in sewers, manure pits, and the like.' Scobie took a breath, obviously reading from notes. She continued.

'And because it's heavier than air it can collect in low-lying and enclosed spaces. And it's a corrosive of copper in certain instances. Copper alloys however are vulnerable to active corrosion by chlorides. So you see these circular sorts of chemical reactions occurring. Pathologist included a lot of chemical analysis but the gist of it all is that she found some green staining of the wrist bones on the left hand and similar staining on the thoracic vertebrae. Suffice it to say the copper which caused the discoloration is no longer present. But the residual staining is suggestive of jewellery.'

'Jeez you coulda precised that lot.'

'I know you can keep up. Be flattered. Oh, and she had some other interesting things to say about rubber, you know, the gorilla mask. She said rubber is a perplexing material when studying its decline or breakdown. She suggested that seemingly identical pieces under the same conditions can react totally differently.'

'Must be a forensic pathologist's nightmare,' Cal said.

'One object may deteriorate into a soft, sticky material. The other may become stiff and cracked even within the exact same environment. Plus, unlike most other materials rubber tends not to be adversely affected by chlorides. So, the very thing that was probably affecting the copper on the body of our victim had little influence on the rubber mask.'

Scobie sighed, took a breath, began again.

'Anyway, combined with her findings we've narrowed a possible time frame for the stowing of the body. The manufacturer says the production of that freezer model ended in June '83. Conceivably, one could've kept working for more than a decade but the motors pack up. The frames and metal walls rust out with leaks. People generally replace them rather than repair them. Obviously, they get manky after that long. And it's not too expensive to get a new one. So, the thinking is that this one may have been buried in the mid to late nineties. Probably not much later than that.'

'That means your missing persons search is going back maybe twenty-five years?'

'That's right.'

'And what if it was someone who was never reported missing?'

'That's absolutely a possibility as well. Very difficult. Not to mention, they could be from interstate.'

'But generally family or close relatives would follow up if that were the case, yeh?'

'Generally. Unless it was someone estranged from their family.'

'Anything else? The hair in the mask?'

Hair can last a long time. It's been found in archaeological ruins. Keratin is tough.'

'Sounds promising.'

'Mm. Well even if there were hair roots they'd have to be fresh to be useful and even then they'd only give mitochondrial DNA. There are advances, expensive procedures, protein markers and what-not. It's possible through several means to match an individual to a hair sample.'

Cal caught on.

'If Richmond Police had that kind of budget.'

'Exactly. This is still a very tricky case.'

'Well, I know this is awkward for you,' Cal cleared her throat. 'I really appreciate you keeping me in the picture. Thanks for letting me know all this. Talk soon.'

'Don't make me regret it Cal.'

Scobie's tone was somewhat light but her point was made.

Cal squirmed at that last comment as she pocketed her phone.

She unfolded one of her topo maps. The Lyrebird track certainly had plenty of offshoots but essentially it ran north-west through the hinterland for hundreds of kilometres before reaching the flat lands north of the Hunter region up near Myall River.

It seemed unlikely that whoever dumped the freezer had come from north to south. Not with vast areas of forest preceding the area it was found in. It seemed way more logical to her that the dumping over the cliff was a rushed disposal by someone from the local area. It appeared someone had panicked for some reason.

The smell came back to her. Her throat constricted as the foul reek seemed to release again into her airways like something she'd ingested and absorbed. She needed to swallow but didn't want the taste reinvigorated by any sort of movement. Whose remains, were they? That had been a body, a person. And who would do that? Shove someone into a small freezer and dispose of them that way? Scobie had said letters were scratched on the inside. *Jesus. By someone stuck in there?* She shook her head, tried to sever the run of thoughts. A stampede of heat raged through her insides as bolts of sparking electricity fired randomly inside her skull. Needed to break out of her own body to escape the claustrophobia. Anything to halt the images and crushing dread.

She was literally panting. Made herself breathe deep and slow. Gathered her thoughts. Went back. *Who would do that?* Someone with a lot to lose if the remains were found.

Mid to late nineties from what Scobie had indicated. Twenty-five years or so ago that freezer could have been buried. And why the hell did they decide to dig it up?

Just as she had with Phillip Leuwins she felt compelled to uncover what had happened. Her shoulders dropped and she huffed out a steadying breath. Dear Pip. Just months ago, on Boarback Ridge, she'd been the one to find her old friend, not realising at the time the remains were his.

She clamped her teeth and stared up at the sky.

It wasn't coincidence that she had discovered both bodies. Of course her job made it more likely that she was exactly the person who would trip over such macabre findings. The amount of time she spent in the area was greater than any hiker, no matter how avid. But time and proximity ratios aside, Cal felt almost chosen by her sad, gruesome luck. It was no accident. Her tenacity and a driven sense of personal duty meant she would pursue what had arrived in front of her until she had satisfied the obligation she felt.

Two and a half decades ago, give or take a few years. What was going on then? Who lived in the area now that might know or remember something? She worked in the area. But she was a relative newbie. She didn't grow up there, didn't have that kind of history with the place. Were Scobie and the team interviewing the locals? Must be. What could she do herself? How could she poke around and dig stuff up? Who would talk with her?

***

Scobie felt slightly antsy having revealed the latest forensic information with Cal before her morning briefing with the squad. But the files had come in late the previous afternoon and the morning briefing would also include an initial report back on completed interviews and Missing Persons. Scobie knew she'd have little chance of bringing Cal up to speed once Cal was out in the field. The fact that she shared any information at all with Cal was highly irregular and the singular blot on Scobie's otherwise stainless character. That and the uncanny level of rationalisations which accompanied the occasional lapses concerning her lover.

She gathered her paperwork and walked quickly to the Incident Room.

At the end of the lengthy briefing an item was finalised for the media liaison staffer to slide to the press. It included an updated time-frame for the Lyrebird Track homicide. Police and public focus were now firmly on the mid-nineties.

Chapter 13

CAL'S RECENT FIND WAS troubling and repeated visions of the day on the Lyrebird Track disturbed her nights. It wasn't that the images as such scared her. It was the horror of what someone had done to a young woman. And that no one seemed to know who this young woman was. She must have belonged to someone and have a family somewhere. Why was she not even registered as missing? Then there were numerous others, the police Mispers list. The endless, always-being-added-to roll-call of missing women. It was alarming and not a new thing nor a geographically specific thing. It was universal, ubiquitous and lengthy. The specificity of this one girl plus her link to the many. Cal felt swamped.

She got up and refilled her glass at the tap, nudged back the curtain at the window above the small sink. The night sky was cloudless, a three-quarter moon cast deep charcoal shadows in the yard.

She'd found the body. Of course, it was upsetting. It was in her head now, that years past a young woman was killed and her body was hidden, and in all that time no one seemed to have noticed that she was missing. Did that mean she wasn't local? And if not, what was she doing in the area? Hiking? Visiting someone?

There wasn't any seasonal work there at Three Rivers. Maybe over in Windsor, fruit picking. But still.

If it was confirmed that this young woman was killed decades ago Cal thought, then what were the specificities of life then? Her own memory was amorphous with dates. Was it before mobile phones maybe? The internet? She could do an online search. Were people backpacking then? Was that even a thing? What was that young woman doing in that region on her own? She must've been on her own. Or someone would have reported her missing. Unless she was with someone and that person was the one who did away with her. Was that it?

She couldn't get back to sleep. After pottering about her cabin and sorting out some long-overdue tidying up she had an early breakfast and set-off for work.

She was on her rounds checking track maintenance, south of where the body was found on the Lyrebird Track. About five ks as the crow flies.

At O'Rourke's Dam Track she parked in the shade on the eastern side of the carpark where the bush protected her truck from the morning sun which was already baking the gravel surrounds. From the rear of her truck she gathered a selection of hand tools and put them into a backpack. She stashed two water bottles, one on either side of her pack, before shouldering it and setting off on a maintenance reccie. Several hundred metres beyond the track entrance she saw a figure crouched mid-trail retying her bootlaces.

'Hiya,' Cal called.

'Oh,' the woman startled.

'Sorry. And I was trying to avoid giving you a fright. So much for that then.'

'Just a bit jumpy. I'm not usually like that.'

The woman stood and dusted her hands off against her shorts. She was medium height, a sinewy build. Her hair was deep chestnut, corkscrew curls that bounced as her head came up. She clocked Cal's ranger garb.

'I heard a vehicle in the carpark. I'm familiar with this place, but since that body was found up on the ridge ...'

'I get ya,' Cal adjusted her backpack on one shoulder. 'I was the one who found it. Wouldn't credit it huh.' She cast her eyes downwards.

'No. Really?'

Cal looked up and nodded.

'Well, I'm glad to see someone in a uniform anyway. It was sorta scary.'

'I'm just a Park Ranger,' Cal gave a quick snort. 'And I think that body was a historic death. I mean, it had been inside that freezer for a long time. Whatever happened it wasn't recent. Still I take your point. You'd think whoever did it would have to be someone with local knowledge. Guess that makes you look at folks a bit differently ay.' She held her open palm to her chest not sure that a hand-shake was called for. 'I'm Cal Nyx by the way.'

'Tyra Huber,' the woman said then gazed across the endless surrounds beyond the scrub lining the track side, rolling ranks of grey-green forest that hazed into the distance in all directions.

'Maybe someone drove here from a long way away. Looked on a map and thought, middle of nowhere. That'll work. I mean, we've all been thinking about it. Everyone's talking about what might have happened.'

'Maybe. Kinda risky to drive all this way from somewhere else with that sort of,' Cal paused, 'cargo … whatever.'

'Listen to us. The amateur sleuths.'

'People love a mystery don't they, trying to figure out the puzzle.'

Tyra Huber brushed the back of her hand across her forehead.

'Well, the stakes do seem kind of high, a body in the bush and all that.' She unclipped a water bottle from a small backpack, took a swallow.

'So, you're a hiker?' Cal said. 'A local too?'

'Mmm hmm. Not born and bred but been here a while. Married a local. Pedro does the maintenance at Three Rivers. I run the B'n'B. Get away out here when I can.'

'Well, I'm sure we'll be running into each other again. Nice to meet you.'

'Same. See you.'

They moved off in opposite directions.

Local knowledge Cal pondered not for the first time. That was the key to this thing.

Later when Cal had finished her reccie and was packing away her gear at the carpark, her phone burred. Dif.

'Hey mate.'

'Sorry to bother you Cal but I figured you'd want to know. I'm just back from the Medical Centre with Spike.'

Cal stopped what she was doing.

'Everything's okay but Spike got hot welding flux in their eye. The cornea is damaged but should heal. They've got an eye-patch on. Just wanted you forewarned.'

'Jesus. Why weren't they wearing fuckin goggles?'

'I know. I've told them enough times. Can't be too hard on them. They had the helmet on but flipped it up to chip off the flux. Don't think they'll forget to keep it down after this. I feel terrible.'

'Don't mate. We both go through all the safety shite with them. That's all we can do. Least they're not gonna lose their sight. Thanks for letting me know.'

'I'll give Spike a hug from you shall I?'

'Let's not go overboard.'

'Later then.'

She ended the call then noticed she had a missed call from earlier. Suzette. Phone hadn't even rung. Bloody dodgy service. She called back.

Suzette owned a small rural property on the mid-north coast. Somewhere Dif and Cal had shared old times. Dif had landed at the place more recently when escaping danger at his camp by the South Coast quarry.

Suzette answered, 'The Ranger who goes where none before her dared.'

'Oh dear. What can I do you for mate?'

'You know you're kinda famous now, right?'

'Hardly. They give a name attribution in a couple of online rags. Not something I sought either by the way. Just doin my job n'all that,' putting on a fakey humble oh-shucks tone.

'Well, notwithstanding all that, up here we've noted it was you referred to in the news as the intrepid ranger who found the freezer. And I had a coffee yesterday with Sierra Gambel and she had something rather interesting to say. I thought you might like to hear it.'

'All ears.'

'She said when she heard the news item about the body in the freezer, what struck her was the name Three Rivers. It's not on the main route south to Sydney.'

'It's not on the main route to anywhere, 'cept maybe back of beyond,' Cal said.

'Well, exactly. You don't just turn off and you're there, right? It's a ways inland on the Hawkesbury watercourses. Kinda circuitous. I looked at the map after I spoke with Si. Anyway, thing is, Si said back in the dim, dark past, she had a fling with this young traveller. A Dutch woman who was at the Wanderground for a bit. It never would have registered but for the name of the place, Three Rivers, and the time frame the police have given. Mid-nineties. Like, it's so off the beaten track and Britta, this young woman, was headed there. I know it's kinda random. Probably best if you speak with Sierra yourself. She can fill you in more. Don't the police always say, no matter how insignificant you think it is, they want to hear about it? Anyway when we saw it was you who found the thing. Well, y'know, hence this call.'

'Sure. Might be good to hear what she has to say.'

'You still have an 'in' with the copper?' Suzette snickered.

'Shut up.'

'Sorry. I guess this isn't a funny matter. Must've creeped you out.'

'That's it in a nutshell.'

'And you're still getting over losing your lovely aunt. And that old friend who died in the bush.'

'Murdered. Pip was murdered.'

'Of course. Sorry Cal. I've been insensitive.'

'All good,' Cal verbally waved it off as a rising dread threatened to engulf her. 'Hey, best get on ay. Let me have that number and I'll speak with Sierra.'

Suzette duly complied.

'Okey dokes. Whatever comes up I'll be passing it onto the coppers too. Or Sierra can ring them herself. I'll tell her that. Be in touch then mate. Have a good one.'

Much as she wanted to follow up immediately, especially since she currently had three bars on her signal, she was supposed to be working her ranger job. Later, she promised herself, curiosity like an insistent prickle in her sock.

Chapter 14

Dusk was descending as Tambor parked about two hundred metres from the alley entrance in Petersham. The light from the setting sun cast the warped timber fencing that lined the back lane in soft peachy tones, at odds with the rubbish and debris gathered in the gutters. Tambor finished his cigarette and walked slowly towards the mouth of the back lane where he paused and peered along the accessway. A broken wheelie-bin was propped lopsided against the nearby fence, the waft of molten bacteria and rot drifting past his nostrils.

Tambor surveilled the alley whenever he could spare the time, gauging the movements of Dif Stangler. Sometimes that other one was there too. Cal Nyx. Also receiving plaudits from the police higher-ups. Publicly anyway.

Tambor lit another ciggy and watched as the freak, Stangler, worked in the dusk dimness fifty metres beyond. A vehicle was pulled part-way into the lane, its rear lifted on a trolley jack. Another character – smaller, younger – was doing something in the boot while Stangler twiddled with a ratchet from underneath. *Ahh, the freak's recruiting now*. He drew deeply on his fag. The smaller character disappeared momentarily then a fan of light illuminated the work-area. *Best wait til It's alone then*. He tossed his fag-end into the gutter. Still, it was a haul from the South Coast to Sydney's Inner West. Might be better to make his impression felt now-ish.

The smaller one had disappeared but then minutes later in a change of clothing had exited the garage and strolled off down the alley away from where Tambor was stationed. Stangler lay on the driveway beside the vehicle, his head under the car body and a corded tool in his grasp. The oddball had ear-protectors on. A high-speed whine scratched through the air as a shower of sparks arced across the asphalt.

Tambor made his way towards the worksite. He reached Stangler, stood beside him and pressed his shoe-heel into Stangler's inner thigh.

Stangler jerked and the tool bounced against some other metallic structure underneath the car, the whirring grind now at a lower pitch. Stangler swore and rolled sideways, his thumb releasing the power switch as he crabbed out from under the vehicle, gazing upwards.

'Remember me?'

Stangler stared at Tambor, held the tool in his grasp, inert.

'Bet you've no idea of the strife you've caused me. Or maybe you do. Maybe you have a very clear picture of the pedantic fucking attention you've brought down on me. The studious regard now riveted my way. Yeh?'

Still nothing from Dif.

Tambor did a quick scope around him. He lifted his foot.

'Get up,' he said

Dif rose. The tool dangled from his hand.

What damage might an angle-grinder do as a weapon? Tambor considered as he noted its presence. Fibre-discs weren't designed for flesh. Would probably just bounce off or only cause a mild abrasion.

He poked a finger Dif's way.

'Rest assured I don't appreciate the interest I'm getting. And you can make it stop. You can withdraw the complaint. Tell them that you lied about the note.' He slammed a palm into Dif's shoulder.

Dif stumbled backwards, a forearm fending Tambor's wrist away as he backed against the fence.

'Piss off,' he finally spoke.

The voice was nearly a whisper but the intent behind Tambor's words produced a grating tone, 'I mean it you fuckin deviant. Think you're a law-unto-yourself you fucking oddball. You call off the dogs. I've seen your new little buddy there. Don't think your young bestie could fight me off. Whaddaya reckon?'

He underlined his question by making a half-closed fist. His knuckles snaked out then retracted in a flash. They caught Dif's head above his ear. Dif's skull struck the wooden fence palings and bounced off. Pain pulses ricocheted inside his skull.

'Do it,' Tambor snarled as he turned and disappeared back down the alley. As he did so he caught sight of the

smaller character's reappearance from the opposite end of
the accessway.

Chapter 15

IT WAS LATE IN the day. Cal was tired and hungry. And she was using a chain saw. Again. Momentarily forgetting this wasn't a recipe for tranquility and positive outcomes.

She just wanted to clear the last of the storm damage from earlier that week. Get it done. Get on.

That was her rationalisation when realising an explanation would be called for. Not necessarily from her boss. Nor so much from Dif and Spike. Scobie would be the scrutineer par excellence.

The fallen tree was resting on another fallen tree. It was pivoting one might say. At equilibrium. Finely balanced. And Cal Nyx, tired, in a hurry, chop-chop-chopping, didn't give the requisite appraisal of the situation. This, her self-recrimination after the event.

Nyx and her trusty Stihl, zzztttt, zzztttt. Cal-I-don't-even-need-to-think-about-this-I'm-such-a-gun-Nyx. Mm hmmm.

Limbing branches and bucking the trunks into logs. Mindless. Slicing through the topmost tree. Zzztttt.

The finely balanced weight and tension suddenly upset and released in a nanosecond as wood fibres once holding hands released their grasp on one another. The weighted limb sprung in an upward trajectory at the speed of sound, not light. Cal's head in the pathway of the rocketing trunk.

Lucky it didn't take her fucking head off, a later summation.

She heard the crack. Was it the tree? Was it her skull? A facial bone? Maybe both. The pain was instant. The swelling, instant. She dropped the tool. Flicked the power switch off. Holding her face. Only the noise in her head, in her ears and the feel under her fingers. *Ahh fuck, what have I done?*

Back at the work truck. Should she look in the truck mirror? Or not? Was she imagining how big it felt. *You idiot.*

Later at Kurrajong Scobie had dropped by for an after work catch-up. She called out and knocked on the door of the old shepherd's quarters.

Cal had kept her head down and her back to Scobie as she filled a glass of water at the sink. Scobie came up behind her, pressed against her back.

'Now, don't get a shock,' Cal said, turning quickly to terminate any potential for spiralling scenarios.

'What on earth happened?' Scobie held Cal back from her, hands on Cal's upper arms as she appraised the duck-egg-sized lump, purple swelling and disappeared eye.

'Had a bit of an accident.'

'Christ Nyx. Have you been to the hospital?'

'I don't have time. What are they gonna do anyway? Want a cuppa?'

'Well, just quietly Cal, they may save your eyesight. You bloody nong.'

'My eyesight is fine. Look, I can see you. You're wearing ... next to nothing actually. Go and put some clothes on.'

'Don't tell me what to do. And don't change the subject. Looks like a broken eye socket.'

'I did hear a crack inside my head. But I can't feel any jaggedy bits.'

'Of course you can't. Your body has filled the area with fluid from broken blood vessels. You're so bodgy.'

'Whaddaya mean?'

'What is this ridiculous survivalist, DIY mentality?'

'I don't have four hours to sit in A and E. I'm sure I don't need a plate in there or anything –'

'Oh, you've given yourself an X-ray, have you? Got a portable cathode ray in your Leatherman knife?'

'Coffee?'

'Yes.'

'I was cutting fallen trees. I was tired. Stupid. Stupid. Stupid.'

'Now you're talking.'

'Have a pew.' Cal indicated the small kitchen table as she filled the espresso pot.

'Think I need to stay upright,' Scobie demurred.

Cal flicked on the gas ring under the coffee pot, turned and leaned back against the bench, her bad eye turned slightly away from Scobie's view.

'So, anything more from forensics?'

'You do want me for my body, right?'

'Only and always.' Cal swooned and made a ga-ga face.

'You don't just keep me on so you can extract privileged information that assists your own hobbiest inquiries and public glory, right?'

'Hobbiest? Really?' Cal turned and unhooked a mug from a shelf over the bench. 'My delvings, Scobes, are a little further north of Amateur Hour I would have thought. You know it winds me up when you get all officious don't you. I mean, I might lose control here.'

'You're an idiot Nyx.'

'You love it. Now, I repeat. What can you tell me?'

'Do you ever wonder why I'm so easily swayed into passing on this stuff?'

'I don't need to wonder. I'm a great fuck.'

'You're beyond belief.'

'C'mon, you know you want to share. Gimme the latest.'

Scobie loosened the clasp at the nape of her neck, shook her hair out. 'The soil samples from the underside of the freezer. They're alluvial,' she raised her eyebrows and waited for Cal's response.

Cal paused then said, 'Laid down by water. We already know it was moved. Somewhere on river flats then.

Lyrebird Track is all sandstone. Had to be on the flats anyway if it was buried, right?'

'Seems that way. At least we have confirmation now.'

Cal nodded thoughtfully. 'Oh, by the way. I had an interesting call with Suzette the other day. Still need to follow it up. But it may have some relevance to your case. Don't wanna muddy the waters as yet but suffice it to say the woman has left her details with your squad's info line. I'm also gonna speak with her, so, one way or another, you'll be hearing about it.'

'So, you're muddying the waters anyway by mentioning it?' Scobie knitted her brows.

'Yup. That's what I do.'

The espresso pot began to hiss on the gas ring.

'You sure you want this coffee?'

'Yes please. Might be a booty call but I still have to drive home later.'

'Yes ma'am.' Cal poured the espresso. 'So, where to next? The inquiry I mean.'

'Well. It's not as though we can canvass the locals asking what they were doing sometime twenty-five-odd years ago. It's crazy.' Scobie said quietly.

'Yeh, it's a long time. Who's going to remember anything?'

'Exactly. People tend to come up with sightings or occurrences once it's been established a crime has taken place. It's an event, something shocking. It sharpens awareness. But that's when the happening is contemporary. Hours, days, sometimes even weeks ago, but not so much. We haven't a hope with something like this. It's such a conundrum.'

'Plus, it seems no one even knew a crime had taken place or even that someone was missing.' Cal touched an itch on her cheek then winced.

'Except for the person or person's who did it,' Scobie said.

'Yeh.'

'Or maybe someone saw something, and didn't realise the significance.'

'Okay, sure. But what we do have,' Cal held a finger up, 'is the freezer. That's been moved and that's in the here and now. That's the link that could unravel everything. Who would move it and dump it unless they knew what it contained? It was a criminal act. It's got to be the person who committed the crime or someone else with knowledge of the crime. Either way, whatever happened back in the past, someone is seriously compromised here in the present. We just work with what we have.'

'So simple. So easy.' Scobie held her hands apart and fake smiled.

'You're up for it, DI. This is your bread and butter.'

'I know you're a marvellous asset to the Parks Service Nyx but you make a very good facsimile of a detective.'

'All I need is a badge. Gimme yours Scobes.'

'You'll have to take it from me.'

'Not a problem.'

Chapter 16

NEXT MORNING CAL WOKE late. She gave Banjo some perfunctory chase and retrieve action from the veranda then took off for work. While she still had good signal on her phone she made the call to Sierra Gambel, the woman who'd spoken to Suzette about a young woman traveller from the Wanderground.

'Sierra speaking.'

'Hey Sierra. I'm a friend of Suzette's . Cal Nyx. She said it was okay to call you?'

'Oh. Yeh sure. Hang on. Just put the dogs inside. Just got home.'

Shuffling, panting, doors opening and closing.

'Phew. Coolios. Okay. Just getting my head into the right space. You're the ranger, the one who found the body. Do they pay you enough for that stuff?'

Cal made a small cough.

'Well, generally I love my job. But yeh, I guess it's one of the downsides. And my patch has been a bit too popular for this stuff lately. Just gotta deal with it ay. So, Suzette said you had some input about the whole situation. Have you spoken to the police? They usually have a Helpline or Missing Persons Register for information from the public.'

'Yeh. I did leave some info on that register. I may follow up with a call. But I just thought since Suzette knew you and her links with the Wanderground. I just wanted to speak with someone who might have a familiarity with the place. I dunno.'

'It's fine. Just go ahead with what you want to say. I can pass it on to the lead detective as well if you think it needs a nudge.'

Sierra took a deep breath.

'Okay. There was this young Dutch woman, a traveller, a backpacker I guess you'd call her. Her name was Britta and I met her at the Wanderground in the nineties. We had a bit of a fling. As you do. Lasted for a few months. She really loved being up there. There were some feral horses in the bush up that way and she was just enamoured with them and I think they were part of the reason she stayed so long. Anyway, her money was running out and there's not really any work up around here. Same back then. She planned to head down to Sydney and get some cafe work before moving on and exploring more of Aus. So, that was the plan. And she'd also talked about finding the grave of a long-ago relation who lived in this part of New South Wales called Three Rivers. It's not a place I've heard anyone refer to before or since except when the news reported it being the nearest town to where the body in the freezer was found. That really struck me.'

'Okay,' Cal said. 'Um, not to be rude but it's kinda arbitrary. How do you know she didn't do what she said and carry on to Sydney and elsewhere?'

'Well, you're right. It is kind of out there. But the thing is I never heard from her again. I mean, it was a fling and all that. But it ended well before she left the Wanderground. Like we were friendly and I thought I might get the occasional postcard or whatever. But I never heard a peep. Not ever again. No one did.'

She took another deep breath and sighed.

'The other thing is the timing. I'm really crap with dates about most things in my life. Big long blurry absences. But there are significant things where I absolutely know when they happened. Britta left here a few days before St Patrick's Day in 1996. I've never forgotten because a gang of our rellies had travelled out here for it and we had a big get-together. I don't have rellies here in Aus. It was the first time I'd met any extended family and I really made some good connections with some of them. It was special.'

'Mm. Well it's definitely worth following up ay. Did you have her last name?'

'This is kinda embarrassing. No I didn't . A lot of women there used different names, rejected their family names. It wasn't unusual to just be on first name basis, no matter how intimate we got. Sorry.'

'No worries. It's good of you to reach out via Suzette and I'll make sure I pass this on to my police contact as well.' Cal envisaged Scobie's raised eyebrow at that description and how on the edge of over-stepping she teetered. 'They may want to speak with you again. Okay if I pass on your number?'

'Course. Hope it helps. Hope I'm wrong too, but I just had to say something.'

'All good. I'm really glad you got in touch. You never know how important it might be, so, thanks. Take care.'

Cal was grateful and humbled that a stranger would be so forthcoming. It only added to her sense of duty and responsibility for unraveling the puzzle and the questions surrounding the freezer discovery. She ended the call and carried on to her rounds wondering if the info would lead anywhere or just fizzle out. She stopped at the general store in Wirriga Flat to gas up the truck and parked beside the petrol bowser. She set the nozzle in the filler neck and pulled the pump lever.

The carpark was bordered with bush, the air crackling with heat and the noise of insects, a bristling explosion of life. The cicadas had a distinctly different rhythm to ones in Aotearoa. In wistful compulsion she began humming the haunting notes of 'Pokarekare Ana', the default national anthem from her homeland.

She finished filling the tank and went inside to pay and grab a snack.

As she returned to her truck she recognised Tyra Huber filling her SUV on the other side of the bowser. Cal paused. A local. She needed to speak with locals.

Cal sipped from her takeaway cup.

'Met you at O'Rourke's Dam Track. Tyra isn't it? I'm Cal.'

The woman looked up, held a palm over her eyes to shade them.

'Yes of course. Place has been busy with Police since then.'

'They've spoken with you?'

'I guess they're talking to everyone. Not that many of us really. But we're a bit spread out, must take them a while.'

Cal took a punt.

'Have you got a minute?'

The woman hesitated. The pump stopped and she replaced it in the holder. She looked at Cal.

'Sure. I'm not in a hurry. I'll just go and pay up. Over there, okay?' She gestured at a pair of wooden benches either side of a faded fibreglass umbrella. The umbrella pole was poked through the centre hole of a large wooden cable reel, repurposed on its flat side.

Cal nodded. 'Thanks. I'll just move my truck.'

She re-parked, freeing up the bowser and then wandered over to the seating area where she stood waiting while Tyra paid inside.

Tyra exited the store with a grocery bag. She went to her vehicle and moved it then joined Cal who waited for her to sit first. Tyra placed her hands on the bench seat like stabilising props.

'I remember you said you weren't from here. When did you come to the area?' Cal asked.

'Milennium. Two thousand. Pedro, my partner is local. So, I guess we had an 'in' to the community. Well, it made it a little easier for me anyway. You're still always an outsider in some respects though. Always slightly looking in from the margins when you don't have all the shared history.' She gave a pensive half smile.

'I'm an outsider too. I work all around here, but I don't live here. I'm not from here. Still, I have a deep interest in this case y'know. I feel invested.'

'Yes. I imagine so.'

'Do you remember how things ran here back then? You know most of the peeps who lived here then?'

Tyra Huber nodded.

'For sure. They're looking that far back aren't they. Beyond actually. I heard mid-nineties. It's sort of crazy though. I've been here twenty-odd years and I'm still not fully part of the community. We are, of course. But people never forget that you weren't born here. Anyhoo. You're part of the investigation?'

'Not formally. But I have an association with the Police. And I'm a Ranger so I have some jurisdiction with the area. I'm privy to stuff. I have a personal interest too obviously. Anything that helps get it solved, y'know?' Cal sipped her coffee. 'Sorry. I guess it seems a bit cheeky. When I ask I'm assuming you've spoken to police already. That you're not telling me anything you haven't said to them first.'

'Of course. So, you'd be keen to speak with people who lived here back then? They've sort of pin-pointed the timeline, yes?'

'That's right.'

'You're wanting more informal, anecdotal information from people here. Something at a different level from Police inquiries?'

'You're very canny,' Cal smiled. 'I'm just wanting to get a feel for things. Bit self-interested I know. But this is my gaff and I found the body. I want to know what happened.' Cal shrugged.

'Know what? We have a get together, a semi-regular girls' thing. A book club but not always with books,' she laughed. 'You should come meet us all, pick everyone's brains. They'll love it. We all want to know what happened as much as anyone else. It's a big deal. Everyone's talking about it, wondering about it anyway. Give me your number and I'll get back to you.'

Tyra drew out her phone, unlocked it and opened her contacts, 'It's Cal, with a "C"?'

'Yeh. Great.' Cal recited her mobile number, amazed at how trusting this woman was, always surprised when people seemed open to her.

'Perfect. Best I skedaddle. Nice to see you again.' She smiled and rose from the seat.

'All good. You too.' Cal got up, gave a small wave and walked to her truck.

Chapter 17

The morning following Tambor's visit to the Petersham garage Dif and Spike were at the workbench in the rear.

'What's his problem? Why's he got it in for you? Who is he anyway?'

'Look at me, Spike. C'mon.'

'Do I have to?' Spike shrugged.

Dif feigned a clip to Spike's ear.

'You look excellent. For an old dude. Damn, you'll never let me forget I said that, ay.'

'That I'm old?'

'Duh. That you look excellent.'

Dif looked away.

'He's a cop. He's a nasty piece of work. You see him around here, just scarper.'

'A cop? What's he done? To you I mean?'

'He's got it in for me. Some people can't leave us lot alone.'

'Yeh, but what's he done to you? It's like you two have history.'

'Just leave it, ay.'

'Jeez. Just askin'.' Spike scuffed off.

Dif picked up a heavy club-hammer and tapped it on the bench. He bounced the head, the handle twirling in his loose grip. Pulled his arm above his head like he was about to slam the head of the tool onto the iron vice. Then he slowly dropped his arm down by his side. His fingers released the handle and the tool fell and hit the concrete floor with a dull thunk.

Later that morning Spike mozied back into the garage where Dif was still toiling away on the project car.

'Got a job for you,' Dif said.

'Don't need any more jobs.'

'Excellent attitude, mate. So, if we're re-powering this rig we need to make sure the brakes are up to it. I think the originals should be okay for the job but this thing hasn't moved in years. The callipers and pistons will need a good clean out and the rubber seals will need replacing. You read up on any of this?'

'Negative.'

'Okay. It's pretty straightforward but the pistons can seize inside. Hard to remove. We might need a few tricks. You wanna bone-up on your YouTube vids so you know what I'm talking about. If you try the compressed air method make sure you wear goggles. Brake fluid and eyeballs don't mix.'

'You want me on this now?'

'You're here aren't you? Cover the callipers with a shop-rag when you run the air through. We don't want that fluid everywhere.'

Spike slouched over to the car thumbing through video links with one hand and trundling a 3-ton jack towards the front end of the vehicle.

'And use jack stands.' Dif instructed as he walked to the welding table, a length of mild-steel angle in his hand. 'Don't want that thing falling on your head.'

'Yes, sir,' Spike replied sulkily, eyes still onscreen. Parked the jack and wandered to the shelf under the rear work-bench and pulled out a pair of stands. Returned to the car, leaned against the door studying a video.

'Piece o' cake.'

'Yeh right,' Dif muttered, then more loudly, 'welding!' as he flipped down his mask.

Ten minutes later, a heavy wrench clattered across the floor and stalled near where Dif was working.

'Hey!' He turned angrily towards Spike who was crouched beside a partly dismantled front brake assembly still attached to the rotor.

'What are you playing at?'

'This piece of shit. Can't get the poxy thing off.'

'Well don't throw tools around the workshop Spike. Y'know, dangerous.' Dif held his hands up near his shoulders, exhibiting about as much anger as a zen master. He took off his welding gloves and approached the Datsun. Knelt down and grasped the rotor in both hands and tried to turn it. It wouldn't budge.

'Yup. Pistons are seized. The brake pads are jammed on the rotor. You need to release some pressure and try to pull them back. Try releasing the bleeder. Use some CRC first. They're mild steel. Easy to break off. Go really gently. You might need heat too so use the small blowtorch.' He looked at Spike who was unfocussed and wore a despondent pout. Their forehead and cheeks were running with sweat. Not that hot in here Dif thought. Hormonal? Hmm. Or maybe this stuff is a bit much for them.

'Did you eat breakfast today?'

Spike looked away.

'Wasn't hungry.'

'Go and have some lunch. Come back to this when you've eaten.'

Spike disappeared inside.

Dif slipped a cassette from a drawer and inserted it into an ancient spray-painted ghetto-blaster on a shelf. Joe Cocker's *Cocker Happy*. He went back to his welding.

Five minutes later Cal came in from the side door. Dif was cutting a piece of sheet metal with tin-snips at the bench. Cal leaned across him and wound the volume up on 'Feelin' Alright'. Started headbanging.

'Fuckin love this.'

Air guitar abounded. Dif hit in time with a plashing hammer.

'Carole Kaye on bass, check it. Leon Russell goin off. Goosebumps,' Cal beamed.

Dif nodded.

'Sorry. Correction. Artie Butler on piano. Leon Russell did the live version.'

'Don't make 'em like that anymore.'

'True mate. More, more.'

'I can't enjoy it properly with my ears on though.'

'Least you won't go prematurely deaf like me.' Cal gave a gormless smile.

Her phone burred.

A text from an unknown number.

-Tyra here. Sat 4pm our next girls' get together. Join us. 9 Heights Rd, Three Rivers.

Cool, Cal thought as she pocketed her mobile.

Chapter 18

At Cal's Kurrajong cabin.

'Is your hairdryer around?'

Scobie looked up from a sheaf of papers she was reading in bed.

'I just misheard you, right?'

'Doesn't matter. I'll use something else.'

Cal went out to her tool shed and hung a damp pair of boxer shorts on a wire attached to a hook in the roof-rafters. The wire had a film of spray-paint on it. She plugged in a hot-air gun and set it on low, playing the blast across the fabric, twirling the wire back and forth as she did so.

A few minutes later she returned inside and laid the boxers on top of a clean pair of jeans. Scobie looked up from the paperwork in her lap.

'Thought you always went commando? What gives?'

'Doctor visit. Best not to shock her if I need to drop my daks.'

'Good of you.' Scobie went back to her notes.

Cal's visit to the doctor was uneventful, meaning Cal wasn't going to go and have an x-ray as recommended but at least she'd had her broken cheekbone confirmed and no, her head wasn't about to cave in. Hence, in Cal's professional medical estimation, the plan going forward was to carry on as usual.

She proceeded to the afternoon's informal book-club gathering.

Millennia of eroding water and winds meant there was elevated ground above the worn-down flats of the Three Rivers settlement. Precipitous in fact.

9 Heights Road was on a steep loop at the edge of the tiny village, overlooking the river and west into the hinterland. Behind the houses the bush ran north, south and east in vast, limitless tracts. The only breaks in the forest cover, aside from the handful of local streets, were the two main roads into and out of the region that edged the waterways and pastureland bordering them. Cal parked in front of several other vehicles. She pulled on her hand-brake and jammed the gear stick into first as an extra hold.

Earlier she'd imagined explaining her association with the general murder inquiry and her personal belief that community input was critical. That someone local must have seen or known something crucial to unlocking the case, even if they weren't aware of it. Remind the women of the time period police believed pertinent but stress that she herself held the view that events significantly prior to that time could also hold clues.

The women would be enthusiastic but might take a while to warm to the idea that an occurrence they were privy to, seemingly unrelated, could hold the key. Cal would encourage them to give reign to anything from their shared or singular histories that struck them as important or possibly odd in some way. She could take notes, highlight points to follow up later. Sorted. Ready for action she told herself.

She grabbed the bottle of wine and nibbles she'd bought and walked the short path to the cottage. Still wearing her ranger uniform, she'd decided not to change as it hopefully gave her some credibility without being unduly formal with people she'd yet to meet. Dressing in civvies might have made her inquiries too weird.

A side pathway went around to the rear of the cottage through an old latticework arch. Cal knocked on the front door. Now that she was actually fronting she began to feel uncomfortable with what she'd planned. It wasn't sitting so well with her. Her fingers clutched tightly around the neck of the bottle of pinot gris. Thank God she had something to hang onto. You're overstepping your authority she chided herself. She had no right, no power to back her up anyway. It was all self-interest. She wasn't a cop. She couldn't ask the questions she wanted to ask. *Oh god, not now.*

There were experts to seek the answers she needed. They were trained. What the hell was she doing there? Plus she had a lump on her face and the beginnings of a black eye.

The door was answered by Charlie Stone, a tall woman with loosely curled fair hair who introduced herself as one of Tyra's friends.

'Just go around the side there,' she smiled and gestured towards the archway Cal had passed on the way in.

No turning back now.

A platform strip of flat ground had been formed with a low rock retaining wall infilled over the years with additions of rock spoil and earth and compost. A small lawn was laid with seating. Concrete benches formed to appear like natural rock followed the contour of the rear bank against the sandstone. Camomile and thyme and other low-growing herbs grew among the flagstones underfoot, releasing their scents as foot traffic crushed their leaves and stems. Several umbrellas shaded disparate chairs and outdoor tables. Half a dozen women made small groups and all looked up as Cal moved into the gathering. Tyra who'd forewarned the others that she'd invited Cal, now stood and approached, introducing Cal to the other women. Then she invited Cal to address the group herself.

At which point, Cal's brain function seized.

'Cal?' Tyra's voice, concerned beside her.

What am I doing?

'I'm so sorry. I've gotta go. Really sorry.'

She scuttled back to her parked truck and started it. Hands clamped on the steering wheel she took off around the loop road and back down the hill. At the bottom she stopped at a T-intersection with the main road. She gasped for air. *That's right, breathe. What the fuck are you on?*

Why are you interfering in this investigation? What are you trying to prove?

The voice in her head was harsh. She breathed out. Closed her eyes. It wasn't as though she was holding up any traffic in the tiny hamlet.

If she could figure it out, if she could make sense of what happened, then she'd make sense of her own losses. Was that it? Or at least subsume some of them.

And, by the way, you've just created another mess you'll need to mop up.

***

Spike ambled out to the garage, semi oblivious to the clear sky, sunshine, drift of traffic noise from Parramatta Road. Did notice the stray black cat sprawled, unperturbed, catching rays on a folded sack atop the two bags of potting mix Cal had left beside the back wall.

Spike pushed back the garage door and switched on the lights, checking out the dusty shell of the Datsun they'd been working on with Dif. Went to the rear workbench, put on safety glasses, a fibre face mask and ear protectors before starting work on the vehicle. Tandem rark-ups from Dif and Cal had fractured youthful indifference and rash practices for the time being at least.

With a small dual-action sander in one hand Spike ran their other hand over the surface of the rear wing checking the filler applied several days earlier when the welding repairs were finished. Dusty. The thought of dust seemed to suggest aridity and Spike's throat felt gravelled. A bodily thirst like they'd been crawling fiery desert sands for days. What the hell? Didn't I drink something earlier? Maybe I peed it all out. Been peeing a lot.

Noticed their hand shaking, even before a long session on the vibrating tool. Weird. Shoulda had breakfast Spike thought. But I did have breakfast. Come to think of it, I feel kinda spacey.

At which point Spike doubled over dropping the sander on the floor as a pain wrenched through their insides like metal claws pulling through the viscera in all directions at once.

Spike's head hit the concrete floor as the sander burred and bumped against the back tyre.

Chapter 19

CAL RANG SCOBIE.

'Just so you know, doc said my head's not gonna cave in.'

'Well that's a total surprise. Did she send you for scans?'

'Oh, you're dropping out. I'll just move. Okay, best be quick, damn signal. Hey, been meaning to tell you. Got a wee lead might be worth following up. A Dutch traveller called Britta. Mid-nineties. Tell you more when I see you. But your team might already be following it from the Hotline. Don't forget to take a break. Kiss kiss.'

Cal ended the call with a guilty squirm. *Blaming the signal, what are ya?*

Her phone rang again. Tyra Huber.

'Ah jeez,' Cal muttered as she answered.

'Hey Cal. Just wanted to touch base. You okay?'

Cal cleared her throat, peered skywards.

'I feel like a total idiot. Sorry about that earlier. After you set up that get together and everything.'

'It's fine, truly. Look I wanted to let you know, the girls are keen to help if they can. They understand it must be weird for you, that you found the body, but you're not a cop. If anyone does remember anything can I give out your number?'

'That would be amazing. They should pass anything onto the cops first of course.'

Then Cal had another incoming call.

'Gotta take this. Thanks for getting in touch Tyra.'

The incoming call was from Dif.

'Sorry, Cal, but I'm doing it again. I thought you'd want to know. Had to have a bit of a medical intervention for Spike.'

'Not another workshop injury? Jeez, have we made a mistake? Encouraging all the workshop stuff.'

'No, no. Nothing like that. They were in the workshop though when it happened. I found them on the garage floor. I don't know if they knocked their head on the concrete or banged it beforehand or what. No blood.'

'Far out. Not drugs or anything is it?' Cal asked.

'No idea. I just put them in the recovery position until the paramedics arrived. Spike was totally out of it. Like in a coma or something. A bit scary. Guess we'll have to wait and see what they come up with at the hospital.'

'Shit, yeh. Is that where you are now? I'm up to my armpits here. Sorry I can't be more help.'

'No, it's cool. I'm here at RPA. I'll let you know as soon as I hear anything.'

'Thanks, mate. Take care.'

RPA. Royal Prince Alfred. Where Aunty Zin was when Cal took off bush, following a killer. Never saw Zin alive again. *Nice one, Nyx.*

Now Spike was there. *We're not fit to look after the kid. And Dif's dealing with it all on his own. You're doing it again.*

Small electric explosions shot across her brain. A whale tail flip-flopped in her guts and a spiny heat blasted through her chest. *Nah. Not now.*

She took a deep breath and held it in. Closed her eyes. Breathed out. Repeated the actions several times. *Spike's taken care of for now. Dif and I can talk later. Back to the present, Nyx.*

First thought in her head. A young woman called Britta who was apparently headed to Three Rivers. Gotta be looked into. What more could she do? What was actually within her power? If Sierra Gambel had spent time with this woman, others would have too. Speak to them and gather some more memories. Fill out the picture. She needed to get back to Suzette.

She made the call to the landline number. The old technology still had its moment for properties beyond the reach of cell-towers. She got the message service.

'Cal here. Another query for you. Probs best if I speak directly. I'll try again tonight.'

Then her phone rang again. This time it was Dif.

Cal answered immediately.

'How's it going? Any news?'

'Yeh. Looks like Spike's diabetic.'

'Shite. Really?'

'Yeh. Must've gone la la. Spike didn't know about it before so I guess it's kinda lucky I came home and found them. They're stable now.'

Cal sighed like she was releasing more than the air from her lungs.

'That was pretty disturbing. So, education for us all on that score, I guess. Better brush up on Dr Google.'

Dif sniggered, 'I'll bring home some info. We can have a family conference.'

'Oh, that'll be fun.'

It was barely mid-afternoon and Cal felt exhausted. Was this what it was like having kids she wondered. Drama and emotional turmoil in regular doses. Maybe it was just life. She seemed to get enough of that stuff before Spike entered the picture. Still, second time in less than a fortnight.

As she drove off she noticed her tense grip on the steering wheel. She missed the wide, narrow version in her old classic Ford, torched a few months back by a lowlife she had been tailing down the South Coast. There was plenty more to miss than the steering wheel. The fluted chrome centre console, the re-conned engine not long run-in. *Paid a packet for that.* An urge to punch the one responsible. *Oh, yeh, already done that. They had to pull me off him.* Now all she wanted to do was cry. All that work, the attention and effort, gone. She blew air from her lips as she gazed through the windscreen at scrub and forest. She also missed a narrow A-pillar roof support that didn't impede her vision. Modern vehicles, huh. You're tired, hungry and grumpy, Nyx, she berated herself.

Chapter 20

Back in Petersham, some time after Cal's ineffectual meet up with Tyra Huber's Book Club, she got a call from an unknown number.

'It's Lola Ringsell. Hope you don't mind. Tyra gave me your number. Said it was alright to call you. I remembered something. Can I talk now? Are you busy?'

'Oh, sure. Now's fine. Just let me grab my notebook.' Cal rummaged in her rucksack. 'Fire away.'

'You said anything out of the ordinary. I hope I'm not wasting your time but I've never forgotten this.'

'Go on.'

'It was magic mushie season. A group of us were camping in the bush. Most of us wanted to try them but I had a really bad trip. It was horrible. I've never taken any kind of psychedelic since. Ugh. I had flashbacks as well.'

She carried on without pause or prompting from Cal.

'We had a fire and some of the gang had brought alcohol they'd nicked off their parents or whatever. Some had a bit of weed as well. The usual stuff teens get up to. Anyway, we had a billy and we made tea with the gold-tops. I didn't notice straightaway. I felt okay just sitting around the fire, mucking around. I just felt a bit woozy and out of it. I had to have a pee and I went off into the bushes and I noticed I was breathing really fast. Like hyperventilating. I felt all light and fluttery in my chest and the surrounds were kinda weird and bendy, distorted and I didn't like the feeling. I just wanted to pee and get back to the fire. Then I got a bit disoriented because I was kinda seeing and hearing things.'

Cal could hear the tempo of the woman's speech speeding up and her voice rising and fluttering as she recounted the story. Cal's eyes focussed out through the window above the fence-line to the sky. Cloudless.

'I thought I heard an animal grunting or something and I got really scared. I thought: bear. Then I realised there's no bears in Aus. But I was still freaked out and trying to see the fire through the trees and find my way back but my vision was funny. Like I was seeing little fireballs all over and I got panicky.'

'I could hear this ... thing. This ... animal. I glanced back above me where I heard this noise and this monster Yowie bloody thing was above me. This animal thing towering over me when I squatted for a pee. I just pulled my knickers up and ran. It was chasing me. Heaving and panting, this hairy thing pursuing me. His breathing was this ragged, hoarse gasping. Like he'd run up a hill or something.'

'He?'

'Oh. It just sounded male somehow. I dunno,' Lola continued. 'Gives me the willies even now,' she shivered audibly. 'I mean, it sounds so silly. Everyone said it was just a bad trip, y'know, but it was so real to me.' She shook herself as though throwing the upsetting memories off but Cal couldn't see that.

'I took off trying to find the others. There was a bit of moonlight. The trees looked like seaweed. Everything was murky and fluid. God it was terrifying. I screamed and eventually the others came running. My first and last experiment with hallucinogens.'

Cal spoke.

'Jeez. Sounds horrible. Did anyone else see it?'

'No. I know everyone thought I was manifesting some fear under the influence of the drugs. I wasn't though. The surrounds might have been distorted, but this ... thing ... had substance. It was material. It was real. I could've touched it if I wasn't so freaked out. He was real.'

'When was this? What year?'

'Um, it was Bicentennial year. 1988. I was thirteen. I know it's a bit earlier than the time span the police mentioned but Tyra said you'd indicated prior years could be relevant too.'

'Totally,' Cal replied, relieved to hear Lola's voice lower in its pitch, her breathing slowed somewhat. She needed to move the conversation to lighter subjects. It seemed almost vampiric trawling the memories of locals to unearth and revisit potentially traumatic events. *Don't leave her hanging, Cal.* She chose some gossip about the recent burnout practice of the volunteer fire brigade that went a bit awry. They chatted on for five minutes before wrapping things up.

Cal read over her notes, underlined a few passages. Closed the book and bumped it against her forehead.

She wandered from the garage to find Dif leaning against the edge of the back stoop, the fingers of one hand working through the coat of a dark cat. His other hand cradled his phone as he watched a YouTube video.

'Who's ya friend?' Cal asked.

'Meet Donita.'

'Why is that name familiar?'

'Donita Sparks. L7.'

Cal dropped into a bent knee stance and mimed power chords. 'Course. 'Shitlist.' 'Pretend We're Dead.' So fuckin excellent. Whatever happened to them? They shoulda been huge.'

'They were 'uge.'

'Yeh. Guess they were. To us anyway.' Cal looked at the feline wrapping itself around Dif's legs. Its fur was shaggy and black with an off-centre white streak above the eyes. 'Okay. I see the resemblance. So, stray? Or have you coaxed it away from one of the neighbours with food?'

'How can you even think that? I'd never do that.' Dif's tone was seriously indignant and hurt.

'Sorry, mate. Just haven't seen it around before. Guess that's the last of the bird-life we'll see here.'

Dif didn't raise his head. 'No bird-life here to begin with.'

'Right again. Despite Zin's plantings. Neighbourhood must be crawling with feline energy. Whaddaya watchin' there?' Cal indicated Dif's phone.

He thumbed the volume up and held the screen towards Cal.

'What the hell is that?'

'Chicks in a drift car.'

'Sounds manic.'

'It's so cool. Charli XCX. Stunt driver, Sara Choi. So cool.'

'Far out. How'd you stumble on that?'

'Spike.'

'Who'd paint a Corvette pink?'

'Hah. You'll love this one then.' Thumbing swiftly, Dif switched to a music video of Benee's 'Green Honda'. 'Who'd name a numpty Honda 'Steve'?'

'Let the head-banging begin.' Cal demonstrated her best moves.

After vigorous readjustment of neck vertebrae, she panted, 'Excellent chicks. Hey, how's the roadster project coming along?'

Dif pocketed his phone.

'Bit set back after Spike's latest adjournment. They were finishing the body prep.'

'Still keen to get it painted though, yeh?'

'Oh for sure. You want to let them shoot the paint or shall I do it?'

Cal squinted into the sun. 'Seems a bit unfair not to let Spike have a go. They've done all the grunt work on the prep. I'm not overly fussy about the finish. No point the way driver's here smash up your duco no matter how carefully you park.'

'They've had a few practice squirts on some old panels. I think they'll be chuffed to do the topcoat, Cal. You going to tell them?'

'Nah. You tell them. You two have taken the lead on this job. I'm just third wheel at the moment.'

'I keep remembering little things, signs I should've picked up that Spike was diabetic. The sweating and stuff.' Dif shook his head.

'Mate. How would you know? Who would know unless they were familiar with those symptoms? So lucky you found them in the garage. Imagine if it hadda happened when Spike was still living on the streets?'

'Eating bollocks food then probably didn't help either,' Dif raised his eyebrows. 'Anyhoo. Spike wants to find a job. Like, a paid one. They've realised DIY is all well and good but you still need some readies for bits and pieces.'

'Shouldn't be too hard here in the city,' Cal muttered.

'I'm wondering if they should get into a trade. Reckon the study side of it would appeal too.'

'Think the engineering crowd are more open-minded these days?'

'Mmm. Don't need to tell you why I ended up being mostly self-taught,' Dif said quietly.

'Listen to us two.'

'I know. It's like parent-teacher night at the local high school.'

Cal guffawed.

'Anyway. Ultimately I guess it's Spike's call. Not really gonna take much notice of us and our opinions.'

'Maybe,' Dif said.

Throughout the day, Cal thought of the call with Lola Ringsell. It was pretty out there. This must be what the police dealt with when they asked the public for information, albeit on a much tinier scale. You asked people to remember things. Who knew how to interpret that stuff, or how reliable it was? Or how factual. How could you verify that anecdotal info? Talk to others who were there? Get a sense of how they saw it. Imagine doing that with every piece of volunteered information. What a mammoth job. *So, Nyx, what are you going to do with this?*

She pulled out her phone, brought up the last unknown call, saved Lola to her contacts and rang her back.

The line was busy. Cal left a message.

'Hey Lola, Cal Nyx here. Thinking about your call earlier. Just wondering if you can remember who else was there that night, at the camp. Do you have any photos from then? Or of the gang or anyone else from that time period? Thanks.' She rang off.

Chapter 21

Spike came from the train station and dawdled through the park where they used to doss in the old band rotunda. Figuring Dif would be working on the car project, Spike didn't use the front gate but went round to the back alley. As they turned the corner beside the broken wheelie-bin, *jeez, when were council gonna pick that up,* they saw a figure dart into the open garage up ahead. It wasn't Dif and the movement was furtive, hunched, like someone reducing their body's silhouette to avoid exposure.

Spike scuttled keeping close to the fenced siding. Got closer to the garage entrance. They could hear a voice, grating and angry. Spike peered around the corner. It was that guy, the cop, standing over Dif. Spike inched closer beside a 40-gal drum where they tossed their metal recycling.

'I fuckin warned you. I gave you an opportunity to sort this and you've done nothing. Do you think I'm a fuckin joke? You think I come all the way up here to sort this because I like the fuckin scenic route? It's not fuckin scenic. And I'm not fuckin funny.' He slipped something from his side-pocket, flicked his wrist. It was a metal baton. He raised his arm.

'Ya fuckin laughing now? Ya fuckin freak.' He brought his arm down. But the crack of breaking bone came from his own forearm. Spike swung a length of steel rebar they'd grabbed from the outside bin.

Tambor yelped and the baton dropped from his shattered wrist. He backed up, spun, lifted his left leg as his left hand grasped his broken right arm. He kicked out at Spike who raised the rebar for another swipe but swerved to miss Tambor's kick.

Dif moved swiftly upright and jammed the heel of his boot into the back of Tambor's standing leg as Tambor had kicked towards Spike. Tambor fell, sprawled on the concrete still grasping his damaged arm.

With the pair standing over him, Tambor paused.

'Get outa here ya mongrel,' Spike growled.

Tambor scrambled to stand. Clutching his arm above the wrist he moved towards the laneway.

'You have no idea what you're dealing with,' he snarled.

'Think you're the worst we've seen? You don't scare us. Just piss off.' Again, it was Spike who spoke and followed Tambor's exit, watching him scuffle down the alley.

Dif came up behind Spike, breathing in shallow gasps.

'You okay?' Spike asked, reaching a hand to Dif's shoulder. 'You're shaking. C'mon. Let's get you inside.'

'Feel useless. I should be able to look after myself.'

'You do look after yourself,' Spike gently placed a hand at Dif's back. 'Predators like him are gutless bullies.

C'mon, I'll make you a cup of bad coffee. That'll take your mind off things.'

As they shuffled inside Spike asked, 'You want me to let Cal know?'

'Not necessary.'

'Okay,' Spike muttered.

Spike filled the kettle at the sink. Dif had sat at the table by the window.

'Much as I appreciate your efforts there, Spike, think I'll be needing espresso. Can you manage?'

Spike hurrumphed.

'S'pose I've seen you two doing it often enough. Guess I shoulda taken notes. You could just keep some Red Bulls in the fridge.'

'Water's fine amigo.'

***

Cal had a missed call and voice message from Lola Ringsell.

"Hey Cal. Sadly, my photo albums from back then are in storage at my folks place. Stuff I didn't get round to picking up after a house move. You've pricked my conscience. Ha. Oops, best be quick. Charlie is the one you want to speak to. She's got pics from way back. She was at the Book Club and she's fine for you to call her. Charlie Stone." Her message ended with the phone number. Cal considered a moment. It felt kind of intrusive digging into the pasts of these people. *C'mon*

Cal, they've volunteered this stuff, they want to know what happened. Just do it, she prodded herself along.

She thumbed in the number for Charlie Stone who answered after a few rings. Cal explained why she was calling.

'Yes, of course. Lola told me. And it's old photos in particular you'd like to see? Why don't you drop by for coffee. Must be close to your rounds to pass my place at some point.'

She gave Cal her address. On the Langdon Stream. It wasn't exactly on her rounds, but she could fudge that.

'Really good of you.' Cal said.

'Not at all. Be nice to have some company. How 'bout tomorrow at eleven?'

'Works for me. Thanks.'

'See you then.'

Next day, Cal parked in an arc of gravelled driveway adjacent to the house. It was a long, low ranch-style build of dark stained boards and was surrounded by bush behind and low borders to the front that grounded the building.

She got out and climbed a set of broad stone steps to the front door and knocked, tapping her boots to free them of grit. She heard footfalls on a wooden floor then Charlie Stone opened the door. She was a tall, strong looking woman, long limbed and straight shouldered.

Cal remembered her from the ill-fated day at the book club and quickly shoved the memory back where it had emerged from least it prompted a repeat attack of imposter syndrome.

Charlie's blonde highlighted hair was loosely clasped at her neck. She held one arm wide, welcoming Cal.

'Nice to see you again. Come on in.'

Cal followed her along a short hallway that opened to a broad living room formed in an L-shape with a large kitchen at one end. A row of floor-to-ceiling French doors adjacent to the kitchen lead out to a flagstone patio of random slabs of sandstone. Beyond that, a lawn edged with shrub borders then the lawn dropped away to the Langdon Stream. Along the banks downstream, Cal could see mounds of earth and flood debris.

'Really appreciate this, Charlie.' Cal followed Charlie to the kitchen where tall stools lined a thick timber slab bench.

'Not a problem. How do you take your coffee?'

'Black thanks.' Cal looked around the room. The décor was rustic farmhouse, exposed beams, warm timber. But rather than the dark timber-paneled walls found in many houses of that style, here swathes of the wall linings were plaster-boarded and painted flat white. Framed paintings covered much of the space.

'You okay to just perch here at the bench?'

'Perfect,' Cal replied, 'You farm here?'

'Nuts.'

Cal looked non-plussed.

'Macadamias.' Charlie laughed, sliding a mug of coffee Cal's way.

'Aha. They like the rich soil, yes?'

'And the rainfall we get here.'

'Doin' it long?'

'Long enough.' She laughed again, somewhat mirthlessly this time.

'That's farming, ay. Twenty-four seven.'

'It is. At least I don't have animal emergencies to worry about though.'

Cal nodded, sipped her drink.

Charlie spoke again, 'Can't help noticing, that's a nasty bruise there. Work-related?'

'More idiot related.' Cal rolled her eyes and looked away momentarily.

'Hey Charlie, Lola Ringsell told me about this weird thing that happened back in the day. It was a bit earlier than the mid-nineties.' Cal described the magic mushies camp-out and Yowie incident.

'Oh yeh. I remember that. She was Lola Jacobs then. We were the same year in school.'

'Do you remember who else was there? Better still, do you have any photos from around that time? Lola thought you might?'

'Sure. She did give me a head's up. Hang on.'

Charlie came back minutes later with a plastic covered album. She opened it on the bench in front of them. The cover stuck to the inside pages. She turned over several more pages then angled the book toward Cal.

'Here we go,' she said, 'That's pretty much the gang,' pointing a finger as she named them. 'Mitch, Troy, Hugh, Lola, Felix. Gawd, look at my waistline. Kill for that figure now.' She laughed. 'At the back there is Jemma, and … ' she sighed, 'What's his name? Isaac Hurley, that's it.'

'Any of them still live round here?'

'Oh yeh. Felix does the ferry. You've probably met him if you've crossed the river.' She put her finger on a tall, curly headed figure. Mitch is the publican at The Bushman's Rest. He dropped us off with our gear. Older than us, obviously. Troy's his son. Lola married Adam Ringsell. Hugh is a GP in Wirriga Flat, downriver. Jemma's married and living in Victoria I think, on a station. Isaac, I lost track of.'

'Do you have much to do with any of them?'

'Small place. Can't really avoid that.'

'So, you've all known each other all that time, and you've all mostly been here all that time?'

Charlie paused. She sipped her coffee and did a version of the thousand-mile-stare.

'Yeh, pretty much. I mean, everyone goes away for holidays and what-not. Some people move away for good. Hugh was away a bit actually.'

Cal raised her eyebrows.

'Hugh Pinder. He's a GP. At Wirriga Flat. You know how long Med School takes. Plus, he did a stint overseas. Met his wife there and came back eventually. Lives at Glenlow Bridge. Bit posh down there.' She winked.

Cal snapped her fingers.

'Course. I've met him. Car accident last week on the Lower Three Rivers Track.'

'Sounds right.'

'So Charlie, do you remember anything from back then that strikes you as important or odd? Anything at all.'

Charlie held her coffee mug in front of her face. Her gaze went across the room, lingered on artworks then moved to the view outside. After a moment she answered Cal but she wouldn't meet her eyes.

'No. Nothing comes to mind. Sorry.'

Seemed obvious to Cal she was withholding something but she couldn't force the woman to speak. She was also aware Charlie was a woman who lived alone. Excepting matters involving Scobie, Cal wasn't predatory at all, but she had a heightened sense of how she was sometimes wrongly viewed by others. Still, it wasn't appropriate for her to push Charlie for information and it was time to leave.

'Best I let you get on with your day then. Taken up a bit of your time already.' Cal rose. 'Thanks for the coffee.'

Charlie had dragged her thoughts back from wherever they'd traversed.

'Hey, you're welcome. Don't be a stranger huh.' She led Cal back to the front door, waved her off.

Cal started her truck, swept around the gravel curve and slowly left wondering how important or not Charlie's silence was.

Chapter 22

CAL TRIED CALLING SUZETTE again later that evening but not too late knowing Suzette was an early riser with the horses to tend.

'Hey mate. All good in the 'hood?'

'Box o' birds. What can I do for you Cal?'

'I'm trying to trace that young woman Sierra mentioned who passed through up there in the mid-nineties. I know women up there moved around a few informal drop-ins. Not just the Wanderground. Weren't there a couple of hang-outs nearer the coast? Port Macquarie?'

'There were. Marna had an old farm near Lake Cathie. Women used to stay there. Little bit closer to civilisation. And someone had a place in Tallowood. What was her name? She was a Yank.'

'Can't be that many feral Americans from back then surely.'

'She helped put up a few of the buildings on the Wanderground. Most of them were living under rotting canvas prior to her arrival. Fabric doesn't do so well in rain-forest,' she said conspiratorially.

'Who'd a thunk it.'

'She had an old truck. Used to drive a gang out to the beach and they'd overnight there with a bonfire. Tori. That's it.'

'She still lives there?'

'You know I think she does. I saw her in Port not that long ago. Have done on and off over the years so she's not moved on to my knowledge. Most of the others dispersed to the four winds. A fair few are up Lismore way.'

'Reckon you have an address or phone number?'

Suzette laughed. 'Bit of a hike for you up here ay. I'll have a dig around mate. Get back to you.'

'Be great mate. Thanks.'

Later that night unable to sleep Cal stared into the darkness. The conversation with Sierra about the young woman called Britta. Probably a young dyke trying to find her people. Not something you usually did in the back country, right? Freaks went to cities to find other freaks. Wanderground was an exception. Anyway, trying to find your peeps was always a bit of a mission. Being in a minority, a stigmatized minority made it harder. That sometimes necessitated having to act on the down low and being a bit underground. Because being easy to find just aided the haters. Some people reckoned things had changed, things were easier now. Maybe. Cal was skeptical, feeling that any apparent safety was arbitrary. Ditto acceptance and tolerance. Like something bestowed. Where was the dignity and respect in that? Anyway, sanctions granted by legislation were meaningless at the end of a kicked boot. That's what counted. Privilege was invisible to those who benefited most from it and they never relinquished power without a fight.

She swallowed.

Surry Hills. A beer can, thrown full, slams into the back of her head.

Leichhardt. A carload of youths screams abuse as she walks alone late at night.

Glebe. A pair of them change direction after passing her on a footpath, follow her, lean over her, shrieking abuse and threats in a testosterone hysteria.

Menacing. Designed to intimidate.

And then there was the actual.

No. Let's not step into that territory of memory.

Focus. Britta was queer.

Cal knew the terrain. Knew what that was like trying to find your people. Knew that, back in the day, the safe places were few and knowledge of their whereabouts required a way in. Word-of-mouth. If this young woman had diverted to the Hawkesbury, where in Sydney was she heading to?

Chapter 23

CAL WATCHED AS DIF served himself some chilli mix then put the frypan on the bench beside the sink.

'Don't you soak that skillet.'

'Cool it hombre. Think I don't know how to look after cast iron?'

'Oh, that's right, you were a hippie for a time, huh. I look at that urban edge in how you combine your duds and I forget your feral underpinnings,' Cal sniggered.

'Well I may have been living a bit feral but it never changed my aesthetic even when I visited the bush. Ask Suzette.'

'True enough. I've seen the photographic evidence. Still, you didn't actually cook there did you? Billy tea over a fire doesn't count. Were you doing it with some bushie Nigella or something?'

'God you're uncouth,' Dif muttered.

'The ladies like me that way.'

'Newsflash: no, they don't.'

'Piss off.' Cal laughed. 'Wanna cawfee?'

'Yeh, go on.'

Cal emptied grinds, refilled the pot and set it on the burner. She leaned back against the bench, her hands behind her.

'Hey mate remember when you first came here, from Un Zud.'

'Mmm,' Dif murmured as he scratched paint from a corroded wire connector over a wooden chopping board.

'And by the way, nice to see you looking after Zin's old formica surfaces there.'

Dif looked up, a closed mouth head-shaking squint at Cal.

'And remember not long after setting your booted plonkers on these fair shores you got a little wayward and Aunty Zin was none too at ease and you disappeared for a bit and sorted yourself out. For a time anyway.'

'Mmm.'

'And it transpired that you were rather close by, in a household of freaky sisters.'

'Get to the point, Cal. And pour my coffee please. I don't like it burnt.' Dif carried on with the wire.

Cal pulled a face and mimicked Dif 's "I don't like it burnt" in a childish grimace. She grabbed mugs from hooks under a cupboard, poured and sent one Dif's way, the sugar bowl following closely behind.

'Well those old chicks you stayed with, they were like a half-way house hippie commune thing for women coming down from that land up the line weren't they?'

'Pretty much. What did they call it?' Dif looked up, a small frown between his eyebrows.

'The land up the line you mean?'

'Yeh.'

'They called it The Wanderground.'

'Right.'

'So the place round the corner, the big house commune thing. Did that have a name too?' Cal asked.

'Not to my knowledge.'

'A couple of those women had been there for over a decade hadn't they? Can you remember any of their names?'

Dif coughed a gentle snigger. 'Yeh. Funny old things they were. I don't know what their real names were or if they'd legally changed them. They were anarchist feminists. Glenda Grime and Valerie Vile.' Dif chuckled. 'They were such good value. And they were really kind to me too. Bit older than us Cal. I wonder if they're still around?'

'Wasn't there a Sandra Scum too? Fuckin excellent. Makes me wanna change my name now.'

'You've already got an excellent name.'

'So have you. Freak can dream though. Bit o' fun.' Cal blew and sipped her black coffee. 'I know you were there pretty late in the scene, but still, you reckon any of those chicks are still around?'

'No idea. Why do you ask?' Dif leaned towards the open back door and huffed detritus from the corroded joint with pursed lips.

'It's occurred to me that the young woman, Britta, she could be the body in the freezer. She was one of us.

Y'know family. And if she was I reckon, chances are, if she'd been at the land, especially since she'd come from overseas, she'd need contacts in Sydney where she was apparently headed.' She took a long pull on her coffee.

Dif had stopped what he was doing. He looked at her. 'I see what you're getting at. It was different times. Before us even. When are they saying she must have been killed?'

'Mid-nineties.'

'Definitely fits with how I remember those times. The Bush Telegraph and everything. Women passed knowledge in their own community grapevines. It's hard to imagine a young queer woman coming all the way to the southern hemisphere and not visiting down here. Women from all over went through that place.'

Cal nodded. 'That's what I'm thinking. I reckon this is a lead. Well, I hope it is. Wonder how we could track them down? Can't still be living there surely.'

'Leave it with me,' Dif muttered as he sliced the plastic insulation from a wire with his penknife.

The back corner of the garage now accommodated a recently acquired piece of equipment that Dif had nabbed at a swap-meet. The sand-blaster resembled a small, display cabinet with a sloping glass lid. Dif placed the corroded wiper motor inside the cabinet, locked the lid, then pushed his hands into the heavy-duty rubber gloves that traversed the inside of the box. Watching through the top lens window he picked the piece up in one gloved hand then lifted the siphon gun with other and pulled the trigger. He aimed the abrasive spray over the corrosion. Like magic the rust, pitting and discoloured metal disappeared leaving a satin finish of smooth, dull grey. Almost like new. He turned the piece over, repeated the process then withdrew it from the cabinet.

Cal whistled. 'Like a bought one bro. Reminds me of a time I took an old ute in to a place to get new seals in the master cylinder.'

'Before you figured out how to do it yourself?' Dif said, turning the object in his hands.

'Correct. I came back later to pick up the ute. The guy showed me the shiny master cylinder mounted on the firewall then tried to charge me for a brand-new one. I knew there was no way he could've got hold of a replacement. He'd obviously chucked it in an acid bath then just hit it with some WD40.'

'What a shyster. Nothing gets past you, Cal.'

'I confronted him and he just got real quiet and sheepish. Couple of 10 cent o-rings and he's tryin' to charge me for a whole new MC.'

Dif shook his head.

Cal continued, 'Anyways you got that lookin' good. Nothin' like bringin' a piece back to life huh. Don't ya feel godlike?' She laughed.

'Keep it seemly mate.' Dif blushed.

Chapter 24

CAL UNLOADED REPLACEMENT POSTS, fencing wire, strainer and a tool caddy from the trailer. She was back at the early settler cemetery to do more repairs after a recent washout. Big rains had eroded the soft walls of the river. Soon the remaining graves would be tumbling westwards with the floodwaters, gone forever. The volunteers seemed to be spurred on by their recent progress, heartened into more regular working bees. Much of the area was now visible, grass and weeds low-mown, gravesites and headstones cleared. Bonus for Cal was it made her job easier carrying her gear to the riverside damage furthest from the carpark.

She worked all morning with a long pry bar and shovel removing broken corner posts and strainers, re-siting new ones. She took a break in the shade for lunch heating her espresso on a small camp-stove. A rare, still upright headstone provided a cool backrest. She thumbed through her notifications. Lola Ringsell had texted.

-Had another thought Cal. Drop by for coffee later if you like.

She'd included her address, midway between Three Rivers and Wirriga Flat.

Cal texted back an affirmative.

She finished her tea, stood and stretched. Looked across to the area cleared recently where she'd sat last visit. She wandered over looking for the grave she'd seen then. Found it and read the full inscription this time.

'Sacred to the Memory of Isa Braam

Who departed this life June 5th 1846 aged 71 years'

Cal was no expert, but that name sounded like it might be Dutch. She tried to Google its provenance but her signal had disappeared. Later, she thought.

As she packed her tools away she considered the damage the river had done, gauging out the walls of the bank. The stream bed wasn't more than a couple of metres deep at the edges. It didn't take much of a prolonged deluge to top the edges of the flat land. And this was sandstone. The same kind of water mass on silt and clay would sweep the surrounds clear. Would expose anything buried close to its path.

She heard a vehicle approaching. Somewhat of a rarity on a weekday afternoon. The other side of the river was the more direct access to other hamlets and the city. The vehicle was moving fast, maybe too fast for the gravel surface. Cal could hear the churning roar of tyres sliding and bumping over the corner berms, an engine speed being throttle-feathered out of the curves. A driver used to that kind of surface. She turned her head from the tool lockers and recognised the dark blue BMW SUV slewing out from the bend, straightening, powering past. It was the doctor who'd come that day she'd helped that bloke with a broken leg and a collapsed jack. Cal waved as she pressed her body close to her truck. Dr Pinder raised a finger as he sped past, a grim set to his face. Jeez must be another emergency Cal thought.

She got in her truck and headed off for a chat with Lola Ringsell.

The sun was dropping behind the western ranges and The Lower Three Rivers Track was shadowed and cool. Cal had her window down, glad of the refreshing air.

She found Lola's small, timber cottage with a steep gabled roof on a rise, well away from the water course across the road. Cal drove up the driveway and parked outside a double-bay shed.

Lola stood at the front door as Cal climbed the steps. She was slender, wiry almost. Her bare arms were toned, perhaps by work and her straight, reddish hair was bobbed and fringed in an angular cut. Cal vaguely remembered her from the first book club at Tyra's place but the strongest memory of that day was her own discomfort and hasty departure. Cal's forehead burned as she squashed down a pang of humiliation.

'Nice wee spot,' she said.

'Yeh. Got lucky, huh. Bit of space from the neighbours, too. I like the quiet. Come on in. Get you something to drink?'

'Just water's fine, thanks.'

Lola gestured Cal towards a pair of adjacent sofas beside a wood-burner stove then went through to the kitchen. Place would be cosy-as in winter, Cal thought.

Lola returned with a tall glass for Cal, a mug of something hot for herself.

'So you've been thinking, remembering,' Cal said as she raised her glass.

'Same as everyone else I reckon yeh. Well obviously it's not like we're a tourist Mecca. Not much to see or do here. And we're a bit off the main line and there's not a lot of casual work in the area. None here and very little in the surrounds except apple harvest over Kurrajong and Bilpin.'

Cal tuned in as Lola's breathless delivery continued.

'Travelers weren't a thing then or now even. Not much anyway. That's what was notable I guess. It stuck out. There was this girl and she spoke with an accent. You know that sort of hybrid northern European with a California tinge. She was dressed in hippie backpacker gear, floaty Indian, Balinese stuff. It's like they take a route Downunder via all those usual stopovers. Arrive here with beads and bits of cotton braided into their hair. You remember that sort of look?'

Cal waggled her head from one shoulder to another, not a nod, not a shake.

'So yeh. She was kinda memorable in the way of being someone sort of exotic with her dress and her accent. But she was only here for a short time, couple of days, I think. For a particular purpose then she moved on to Sydney.

There's a bit of early settler history in this region. She was just following up on some relative from more than a century ago. Well you would, wouldn't you. If you'd come all the way from northern Europe. But I'm sure it's in the time frame the police have established. Because I was back here. I'd done some training up in Armidale and finished in ninety-five. I was looking for work and thinking about going overseas for a bit. It was early in the year and my mum needed a break with my brother. He's on the spectrum. Severe. I stepped in for a while and gave Mum some respite. I must've been at the store picking up supplies because I was outside and this girl was sitting in the shade of the verandah eating an ice-block. We chatted for a moment and introduced ourselves. Anyway, since all this has come up, with the body being found, and them saying it was a young woman. I mean I guess it would be a weird coincidence. But we're off the beaten track so.' She shrugged.

'Did she stay with someone here?' Cal asked.

'Not that I'm aware of. Like I said. It was just a day or so. I think she may have camped on the picnic ground near the pub at Three Rivers. There's a grassy flat by the river. Still warm that time of year.'

'Don't suppose you remember her name?'

'I do actually. Sort of foreign sounding. The kind of name that lodges because it's so one-off. Britta.'

Far out. There it was again.

Cal worked at her face remaining a neutral, unreadable dial.

'Did you ever get male back-packers here or whatever they called them then?'

Lola pondered a moment.

'Mm, one time a couple came through. In a van. Y'know, boyfriend and girlfriend. I guess it was the beginning of that whole young traveler movement here. I can't really remember anything specific though. I mean, that area below the pub, it's like a camping area now. But back then it was a picnic area. Used by locals mostly, y'know.'

'What were the blokes around here like?'

'Anyone unhinged you mean? Jeez, Cal. Can't say I've ever looked at anyone around here and thought, "Are you a killer?" Mind you after that Yowie business in the bush camp, gotta say I've always been a bit toey.'

Cal gave a little snort, embarrassed.

'Guess it's a silly thing to ask. As soon as you say it it kinda invites your brain to go into a sort of fantastical overdrive eh. But still that's a really good lead, the name. Have you passed it onto the police?'

'I did. I left it on that phone-in line this afternoon.'

Chapter 25

Spike and Dif insisted on a blindfold, a scarf of Zin's that hung on a rack behind her old bedroom door. Cal had never put them away. Imbued with Zin's scent, Fabergé's 'Babe'. The clove fragrance of her sneaky night-time cigarettes. The remnant floury aroma when Zin opened the cake tin, indulging Cal with treats. Or maybe Cal's memories put those things together when they weren't really still there, not even as atoms of a long ago fragrance. It had all dissipated. Reminiscence the only power, the reality lost.

In the kitchen Dif wound the soft fabric twice across Cal's eyes before knotting it. Putting himself on one side and Spike on the other they lead Cal out the back door, down the steps and across the yard to the garage. Single file they walked her through the doorway.

They'd opened the back roller door and moved the car into the light of the back lane. All its new livery and shine were displayed to the max.

Dif untied the knotted material.

'Okay. You can look now.'

The little sportster had been put back together with different wheels, refurbished bumpers and door hardware. Replacement racing seats, sourced online for a parts-swap, and tarted-up lining of the rear tub, courtesy of another favour with a mate of Dif's.

But the most startling and showy change was the paint job. From undercoat and rubbed back patches the low-slung, topless roadster now bore a coat of satin gunmetal.

'Oh my god. I can't believe it. It looks amazing. Did you spray that Spike?' Cal gushed.

Spike beamed. A rare animation.

Cal looked at Dif, who threw an arm around Spike's shoulder.

'It's so cool. And you've lowered it.' Cal went closer for an inspection.

'Only a little,' Dif said.

Cal walked around the car.

'A lot. I love it. The stance is perfect.' She crouched and eyed along the side of the car.

'Jeez you two. It's straight as.'

She ran her fingers lightly along the surface of the front wing.

'I love what you've done with the bumpers. Is that powder-coated?'

'Something like that,' Dif answered. He and Spike couldn't afford that expense, so they'd done their own version. The effect a muted black, not gloss, had obviously received the tick of approval.

Cal stood back. The wheels were period correct: five-slotted mags in polished alloy. The deep profile and the lower stance of the car gave the impression of a crouching beast, grounded and ready to pounce. The sportster looked updated and improved yet had lost nothing of its classic heritage.

'You two should go into business. Truly.'

Dif and Spike turned to each other, grins growing.

Cal pulled the roadster into the Alexandria back lane and rang Scobie.

'Cmon down. Got something to show ya.'

'Do I need to dress?'

'Might be an idea.'

'Give me a minute.'

It was a balmy spring night and the air was clear following afternoon showers. A scent of early jasmine from a lace of blossom draping the top of a nearby fence promised heat, summer and good times.

Scobie appeared down the back stairs in a tight cotton sheath and a light chiffon scarf at her neck. Cal broke her fug of awe and got out to open Scobie's door. Before Scobie could get in Cal pulled her close, one arm firmly around her waist. She kissed her, pushing her back against the front fender.

'Thought you might like a spin.'

'Might want more than a spin.'

Cal held the door of the topless sportster as Scobie folded her legs into the well.

'Buckle up, sister.'

Chapter 26

SPIKE APPROACHED CAL, WHO was standing at the kitchen sink gazing absently out the window.

'Um, I need to tell you something. But it's awkward. And I don't feel good about it.'

Cal's antenna twitched. She turned and made eye contact with Spike.

'Mm hmm.'

'Do you know that cop, Tambor?'

'Know of him. Why?'

'He's been giving Dif a hard time.'

'What, here? In Petersham?'

'Yeh.'

'What sort a of hard time?'

'Tried to give him a bashing.'

A superheated pulse thumped up into Cal's chest. The muscles in her forearms and hands tightened.

'Why hasn't anyone said anything to me? What the fuck?'

'Sayin something now. Don't yell at me.'

'Sorry. Not angry with you. I'm just wild. So Dif told you this? That doesn't make sense. Why would he tell you and not me?'

Cal felt a weird sense of betrayal. Her mind swirled, her emotions firing off in all directions. She bit her jaws together. *This family isn't your first family. Calm the farm mate.*

'I saw stuff. I was here.'

Spike explained what they'd seen.

Cal was ready to leave for the South Coast, then and there.

'Fuck me. This place is a nexus for unholy shite lately. Do you reckon we need a smoking ceremony here or an exorcism or something?'

Spike shrugged, looked hurt.

'Not you mate. Sorry. Not your fault. Medical events aside. Jeez, I dunno. Think I feel a bit guilty everything happens when I'm not here. Then I kinda overcompensate. Wanna get on the warpath.'

'It's just life, isn't it?'

Cal was pulled up short.

'Where'd you get so wised up? No. Don't answer that.' She scratched the fingers of both hands across her scalp and breathed out heavily. 'You've lived plenty, haven't you mate? I'm a nong. Fuck me. What are we gonna do?'

They were both silent awhile.

Then Cal spoke.

'You're right. This is awkward. I don't wanna be talking about Dif here behind his back and I'm sure you don't either. We need a family conference.'

'You're kidding, right?'

'No. We'll make it a party. You decide what grub you want and I'll sort it. I'll tell Dif we've had a talk okay? You don't have to front him.'

'Nah. I'll tell him. I want to explain.'

'Okay mate. You're right. My ideas are always shite.'

'No, they're not. Party food is always a good idea.' Spike kept their face impassive.

'You're too kind.'

'I gotta get a move on.'

'We okay?' Cal's eyebrows in a small frown of query.

Spike held out a fist.

They bumped knuckles.

Chapter 27

CAL SAT AT THE kitchen table in the Petersham cottage, a coffee mug in one hand. Her phone rang. Scobie.

'Am I going to see you anytime soon?' Scobie's tone was playful.

'I hope so. I miss you.'

'How's tricks Nyx?'

Cal sighed. Her voice lacked energy.

'Frustrated I guess. Not making much headway with anything. Makes it hard to keep going y'know?'

'I do indeed.'

'Course you do. Sorry. How are things your end?'

'Not that I can talk about it,' Scobie laughed without mirth because they both knew she regularly shared information with Cal that was borderline confidential. 'Stymied like you. It's a slog working for that break. The team are being their relentless selves. But yes I certainly have weeks where I wish for a more results-apparent-in-a-timely-fashion occupation. This week would be one of them.'

'We need some fun.'

'No argument from me. Come and show me a good time.'

'I'll apply myself to that one hundred percent Detective Inspector.'

As Cal ended the call Dif shuffled in the back door.

'You seen Spike lately?' Dif said.

'Yeh. Why?'

'Think maybe they're seeing someone,' Dif said.

'Could be, I guess. It's not like Spike's on a curfew or has to check-in.'

'Yeh, I know.'

'And it's not up to us to keep tabs. Jeez, remember what we got up to at that age.'

'Rather not.' Dif filled the espresso base with water, raised eyes to Cal who shook her head.

'True.'

'But I just worry when I haven't clapped eyes on them for a bit.' Dif said, gnawing on a hangnail. 'This must be how parents feel.'

'How the hell did that happen mate?'

'It's a mystery Cal.'

***

Spike heard a tiny whistle and unglued an eyelid. Dim. Tuned into breathing. It wasn't their own. Closed the eye again then felt warmth along their body. Froze. Opened both eyes and scanned the surrounds with more intent. Unfamiliar. *Fuck.*

Fuck fucketty fuck.

Daylight leaking from behind scarves and beads and shit hanging over the windows. Spike sniffed the air. Girlie smells. Faint. Spicy, peppery perfume remnants. Girl's room? Nodded into the pillow while scratching across the inside of their brain for the previous night scenarios. Seeking hours. Locations.

Blurry grey scapes. The occasional flare of zagging colour. No images coalesced. Spike groaned with a mild despair. The body beside them pressed closer. An arm insinuated around Spike's midriff, settled fingers beneath Spike's body.

Lying in the warm, not unpleasant heaviness, a name floated across Spike's brain. The girl. Dylan.

Later.

'You wanna stick around? Have some fun?'

'What kinda fun?' Spike croaked.

'Watch and see. You have to be anywhere?'

'Free as a bird,' Spike lied.

'Let's see you flap those wings then,' Dylan urged.

Spike sniggered. Hid their eyes behind a flop of hair.

Dylan pulled over her shoulder bag from beside the bed. Withdrew a small, brocade drawstring bag from an inside pocket. She opened the drawstring and tipped out a tiny brass casket about half the size of a matchbox. She flashed her smudgy, deep-set eyes at Spike, a grinning twist to her lips.

'Been saving this.'

Spike pouted and raised their eyebrows. Didn't ask questions or reveal possible anxiety, nerves, trepidation.

Dylan flicked a baggie containing white-powder.

'Better brekkie than toast and coffee I say.' She looked at Spike again. 'And don't tell me you don't do breakfast. I won't have it.'

***

At Scobie's Alexandria apartment next morning Cal woke to a coffee mug on the bedside table. Scobie wasn't beside her.

Cal glugged half the contents of the mug. It wasn't hot. She checked her phone. 7-30 am. Scobie was up early. Cal went out into the living area where Scobie had her laptop open and paperwork beside it. She wore earphones.

Cal got into her sight-line and mimed thanks with her mug held aloft.

Scobie smiled. Paused something on her screen.

'Good sleep?'

Cal blinked.

'Well, you ensured that DI. Whaddaya up to?'

'Work. I made you some fruit salad there if you like.'

'Ahh. Bit ... fruity for me. Thought maybe we could go out for brekky.'

Scobie shook her head distractedly.

'Can't hon. Gotta get this done sorry.' Her eyes back on the screen.

Cal sighed heavily. 'Fucks sake. Can't ya give it a break for once?' It sounded harsh, without humour.

'Hey. Don't talk to me like that. What's the matter with you?'

'I'm frustrated. Sorry.'

'Well deal with it.' Scobie moved some papers on the table. 'Actually. Deal with it elsewhere. I'm not up for this Cal. Take it away. I've got enough going on here.'

Cal mumbled to herself. Slump-shouldered she went back to the bedroom and snatched her holdall from the floor, jammed her clothes and charger into the zippered opening and left down the back stairs. She managed to not slam the back door when doing so and thought that was some kind of achievement. Then thought about that as she started the truck and realised she'd not only angered Scobie and undermined their connection and humiliated herself in the process but she'd also corroded one of her few trusted confidantes and sounding boards.

You're a fuckwit Nyx. Your own worst enemy. Whaddaya fuckin doing?

She slammed the truck into gear and dropped the clutch, gripping the steering wheel as the back-end bit into the asphalt.

Why do you do this? You know she's busy. You don't even care about going out to breakfast. You do this shit for no reason.

Sped up the back-alley. Hit the brakes at the end. All clear. Slewed out into the cross-street. Nearly got collected by a flat-nosed tipper truck. The driver blasting her with the air horns. Cal waved an apologetic hand in her mirror.

Jesus Christ. How did I not see that? Get a grip Cal.

She needed a coffee. And she needed to calm down. Well that pairing wasn't going to work. She did it anyway. Stopped at a hole-in-the-wall barista at the bottom of King Street. No one queued in front of her. She gave her order to the cute chick with dreadlocks piled high and wrapped atop her head.

'Double-shot long-black thanks.' Cal eyed the chocolate brownies in the cabinet. 'And one of those bad boys too.'

'Perfect, hon.' The barista twisted the knob over the paper cup.

Cal watched the traffic and tried not to breathe deeply. Diesel and rotting garbage in that heady overheated King Street combo.

What is bugging you Nyx? You feel crap 'cos you're not making headway with the case up the mountains. Is that all? No, it's not. Where the fuck is Spike? I can joke with Dif about what we got up to. But it makes me cringe. Seriously. The number of times I could have clipped my ticket. She shuddered. *It's no joke.*

'Double shot and brownie, hon,' the barista called.

'Thanks.' Cal turned, smiled, and took her take-out.

Her irritation bubbled away as she drove back to the Hawkesbury and Kurrajong, her system zazzing with caffeine and sugar. Maybe there was just too much going on in her life she thought. Spike, Scobie, the upset of finding another dead person. It churned her up, the worry and conundrum of it all.

Things weren't quite aligning. There was something missing. Or something was pointing them in the wrong direction. They should be further along with the investigation. She didn't get it. Either she was missing a piece of the puzzle, or there was a source of obfuscation, something fragmenting the pictures. If she was looking in the wrong place, or at the wrong person or people was that due to a deliberate interference? It could be anything. *Seriously. Do I have to go back over everything everyone's told me?*

Someone at the pub on that last night. But who knew Britta was camped there? Who told her to camp there or did she discover it herself? Did she tell anyone she was camping there? Was that the only place she camped, ie, a one night stay? Why would anyone be lying way back then? Something to hide or protecting someone else? Doing something dodgy.

But it was so damn long ago.

Chapter 28

CAL READ AN EMAIL from Suzette as she waited at traffic lights. When she'd finished she called Dif.

'Bit of an update for ya. Vis-à-vis our convo about those halfway house chicks. Our old mate Suzette has come up with the goods again.'

'All ears.'

It was Suzette Dif had gone to months back when he'd left his South Coast digs under duress. Cal had tracked him down at Wyld Wood, a place from their shared past, somewhere they both felt safe.

Cal continued.

'Apparently Val Vile is no longer around. She o'ded a long while back. Pretty sad.'

'She was a real sweetheart to me. Patient and generous. I'm really sorry to hear that,' Dif said.

'All-too-common story for us lot, ay,' Cal paused then went on. 'The other two, Glenda Grime and Sandy Scum. Not so sure. Do you think it's worth trying social media?'

'You love saying those names.'

'I do.'

'They were anarchists. I can't really see them embracing that stuff.'

'People can change, even their politics,' Cal said.

'Sure. But their names. I never knew their real names,' Dif said, 'That makes it hard too.'

'But if they were trying to be incognito surely they'd use those very nicknames from the past. You said yourself you don't know their real names.'

'Guess you might be right. They'd still be under the radar that way. I have a feeling Val Vile was originally from Brizzy. But you know so many of those women had nightmarish backgrounds. They were escaping their families and their pasts. You don't end up in a feral commune in the whoop-whoops by accident. Y'know? It just makes the job that much harder.'

Cal nodded to herself as she listened then replied.

'I don't imagine those women ever moving back to where they came from for some kind of reconciliation. They were like a diaspora. Could be overseas now, or up in Darwin, WA, Tassie, as far away from family as they could get. Someone must know though. Someone must've kept in touch. People wrote letters, postcards back then. There were group houses.'

Dif spoke up.

'Sydney got so expensive. Those women weren't corporates. I'd be surprised if any of them were still in the Inner West. If they didn't have community housing, I think they would've drifted right out of Sydney or interstate where it was more affordable. If you can leave it with me I can ask around.'

'Sure. Suzette did her best. She's still following up a few old contacts. If you could do the same mate.'

'Will do.'

Cal had no sooner ended the call to Dif when she got another email from Suzette.

"The stuff I've held onto. You're lucky we've been in deluge up here Cal. Can't do much outdoors and your dogged requests forced me to tidy up the storage boxes in the lean-to. Among the ancient uni notes I've now disposed of I also found an old address book. Even have a few landline numbers you could try. Some people still use them huh? I've put out a couple of feelers via email too. Let you know if I hear anything more. But this might help.

"I got an email back from Tori and she got in touch with a woman who travelled with a Dutch woman called Britta. The woman, Shauna Rojas, is in Taos, New Mexico now. But Tori says she's okay for you to contact her. I've attached her email and a mobi below. Good luck. X Suz"

Cal felt a small electrical charge zag across the skin of her neck. The name was the same one Lola had mentioned. Surely it was the same woman.

But her cell connection was inconsistent out on her rounds. She'd have to wait until she could get online at home to call the woman in the States.

Cal studied her topo maps again. She homed in on waterways and there were plenty of them. She was in the Hawkesbury after all. The area named after the biggest watercourse, fed by tributaries all through the surrounding mountains. The maps were riven with the tracery and webbing of multiple tiny, blue lines. Maybe this was going to be a bit harder than she'd hoped.

C'mon Nyx, don't give up so easy. Focus dude, focus.

She took a breath and drew her finger along the Lyrebird Track, moving towards the western end. She circled her finger wishing she had her folding, thumb-sized mini-magnifying glass but it was in a bedside drawer back at Kurrajong. She pinched and spread her index finger and thumb as though she was working on a screen. Then she remembered she did have a magnifier, a small one in her botanical samples kit. She went to one of the toolboxes on the back of her truck and pulled out a heavy-duty plastic case. It was no larger than a small laptop but deeper. She withdrew the magnifier from the same-shaped depression in the dense foam packer and returned to her search. She was good with maps. Could picture exactly where the populated homes and properties were even without markings. Now she could also see the topographical nuances of the areas she was less familiar with, the occasional farms and properties she rarely passed or worked near but were bisected and divided by their own patterns of waterways. Some that may not feature except in flood.

The cogs in her brain spun and meshed. She had a few hunches. She nodded to herself and folded the maps away.

Later at home in Kurrajong after a shower and a snack she checked the time zone for Taos. Sent both an email and a follow-up text message to Shauna Rojas, hoping to set up a call at 11pm that night, 7am in New Mexico.

She also checked the name from the cemetery, Isa Braam. Very likely Dutch or more generally Western Europe. *Holy moley.*

Couple of hours later Cal made the call to the US.

'Hey. Thanks so much for this. Really appreciate your time.'

'Happy to help if I can. When Tori got in touch, I had a poke around in my old photographs. They take up space but what's worse? Unsticking ancient Polaroids or scrolling a screen. I dunno? Should really scan them all for posterity but who has time for that, huh?' She laughed. Her voice was rich and deep and loud.

'So, you knew Britta?'

'Mm hmm. We had a bit of a thing back then. Everyone was hooking up with everyone else. You know how it goes.' Another snicker. 'We knocked around while she was there. Mostly out at Tori's digs. I can tell you what I know. It's not much. And I've got a few images of her then. I could scan them and send them if you like.'

'Great. For sure.'

'She was from Holland. She was at the opposite end of the earth like many of us trying to make a fresh start. Finding out who she was away from her family. You know the scene. I guess lots of kids still do the travel thing. It's an adventure and it's freedom. But for some of us there's a bit more desperation and survival about those kinds of moves, y'know?'

'Totally,' Cal concurred.

'Um. What else? Her family were religious. Followers of a Christian Reform Church, conservative.'

Jeez how's her memory, Cal thought. *That's pretty specific.* Said nothing.

'She wasn't in touch with her family. Disowned because she'd accused a family member of abuse.'

'Oh, that old chestnut.'

'Yeh. Never heard that one before. Not.'

'She had an after-school job and saved what she could. When she left school and reached the age of independence, which was eighteen over there, she took off for the city. Amsterdam. I think the age of majority was younger if you were married.'

'Convenient,' Cal commented.

'For the institution of marriage. You bet. So she searched for women like herself. You know the routine, I'm sure. There was a women's café in Amsterdam, Café 't Mantje near the Oude Kerk.'

'How do you remember this stuff?'

Shauna chuckled.

'When I heard from Tori I dug things out, and I've been thinking on it all y'know. Little tippy-toe down memory lane. That café in Amsterdam, it had closed but was re-opened in 2008. I was in Europe in 2010 and I visited.

Y'know getting a feel for a somewhat significant point in someone else's journey. Those places were important.'

'I hear ya.'

'So via those contacts Britta found a squat near a canal. Can't remember the name of the canal. Walls knocked out. Several floors. Women there from all over Europe. Travellers. And it was there that she heard about this place in Australia, the Wanderground. She worked and saved all she could. In less than two years she made her way to the Southern Hemisphere. As far from her childhood home as she could get.'

'Wow. This is amazing.'

'She must have been twenty, twenty-two when she went to Australia. Did seasonal work to pay for her travels when she got there. She was a sweetheart. Messed up and screwy. Y'know, a handful. She was a lotta fun though. She loved horses. There were feral horses on the Wanderground. She adored them.'

Towards the end of the call Cal felt uneasy about her reasoning for reaching out. She couldn't prove the hunch behind her motivations so why bring the wistful tone down to something sinister and ugly? She felt deceitful somehow. But what if she was wrong? It wasn't fair to destroy this woman's memories if she was misguided. She could always call again if it transpired her guess was correct.

'So, did you know her last name?'

'Good question. We weren't much for that stuff back then. But she was going to that area. Somewhere not in Sydney. On the outskirts.'

'Three Rivers. Hawkesbury,' Cal offered.

'Yeh that's it. Three Rivers. Some genealogy thing. Kuiper.' She spelled the name for Cal. 'A relative. A woman way back. The early settlers.'

'A Dutch woman?'

'I think so. I think that's how I understood it. Sorry. Memory's getting a bit scratchy now. And I haven't had coffee yet.' The throaty laugh again.

'Well, I better not keep you from that any longer. Hey I'd really appreciate those images and if you think of anything else just flick me a message. Nice talking to you.'

'Yeh you too. Makes me feel kind of nostalgic, sad. Have a good one.'

Cal ended the call. Stared off. A runaway from the other side of the world. That made sense of the lack of follow-up. No Missing Person's report. A young woman estranged from a faraway family. A traveller. Loner. Who would notice her gone?

Chapter 29

NEXT AFTERNOON CAL HAD managed with the use of judicious assurances and apologies to land herself in Scobie's "Pending Outcome" column. She'd even wangled a hook-up at Kurrajong which illustrated her not-insignificant prior standing with the woman.

'Think I'm making some good progress here. Last night I spoke to a woman in the US who had a fling with a young Dutch woman who was heading to Three Rivers. Too much of a coincidence to ignore I reckon. The name Britta Kuiper is coming up from near and far. Has it come up with your team?'

'Yes. Still following up. Amongst many other names dropped into our database. Takes an age to process every single one. But we have to.'

'Well I have the advantage of trailing just the one name ay. I'm using my own contacts and it's kind of organic and I dunno if they'd be as forthcoming with police. Having said that, I've been assured by everyone they've left their info on the tipline. Lot of these women don't view the paramilitary, patriarchal brethren as allies.'

'You mean the Gay Liaison officers aren't improving relations in the community?' Scobie's tone ironic.

'Window dressing. Plus, some of us have shady pasts and long memories.'

'If anything firms up from a lead into evidence perhaps the possibility of solving this crime and bringing someone to justice will loosen their reservations enough to speak with us. I get it that you have a way in that we police don't. But we're dealing with a breach of the law that's about as serious as it gets. And I know you know that. I just need to hear myself repeat it to you. In my professional capacity as an officer of the law.'

'You know I go ga-ga when you talk like that.'

'You're an idiot, Nyx.'

Scobie's phone burred. She glanced at the screen.

'Have to take this. Do you mind?'

'Course not.' Cal replied, getting up from the couch. She went to the kitchen to give Scobie some privacy. Filled a glass from the tap and leaned back against the benchtop. She glanced in Scobie's direction.

Scobie's eyebrows were drawn in and her eyes cast down. Her thumb scribed arcs on the surface of the coffee table. Cal could hear Scobie's firm, quiet voice from where she sat. The huskiness had notched up a little.

'I should come down.'

A pause as the caller spoke.

'It's not a problem. You need support. You and Mum both I mean.'

Another pause.

'Okay hon. Just call me if anything changes. I know it sometimes looks otherwise but I'm not married to the job. I can be there.'

Scobie nodded, bit the corner of her lower lip.

'Okay. Lotsa love.'

Scobie stared into the middle distance; her phone still clutched in her hand.

Cal walked over and sat beside her.

'Everything alright, Scobes?'

Scobie was silent a moment. Still gazing off she murmured, 'My dad. My step-dad. He's had a stroke.' She seemed to pull herself back into the room. 'That was Imogen.' Scobie absently tapped her phone against her thigh.

'Oh sorry to hear that. Bit of a shock.'

Scobie put her phone on the table, then her hand on Cal's knee.

'He's a good man. A bloody smoker. Mum must be a puddle. Jesus.'

'You heading down?'

'Imogen thinks I can hold off. God, this is the hard part about being interstate.'

'I didn't realise he was your step-dad.'

'No. I guess I don't talk about it. My dad's still alive. We're not that close but he and mum parted ways when I was fourteen. Norm was an old family friend. He's always been on the periphery. I don't think there was ever anything going on before mum and dad split but who knows, maybe that's just a child's fantasy. Anyway he's a lovely fella and ...' Scobie faltered.

'Oh, darling.' Cal put an arm around her, drew her close, kissed her hair.

Chapter 30

CAL'S PHONE RANG. DIF. She hoped it wasn't another hospital admission for Spike.

'Mate, I've got something I think you need to hear. I don't want to play it over the phone with your dodgy reception out there. When are you due back in town?'

'I'm coming in tonight after work. Or you could send me the sound file.'

'Nah. I'm afraid I'll muck it up somehow. I'd prefer to just play it to you. Do you mind?'

'Whatever works.'

'Let me know when you're on your way.'

'Ten four.'

Later Cal and Dif were sitting together at the kitchen table in the Petersham cottage. Dif sipped from a water bottle. He'd been to visit Sandy Scum, one of the women who'd lived in the semi-commune halfway house in Petersham back in the day.

'How the hell did you track her down?'

'Mate of a mate who's a high up in social services knew Sandra worked in a detox. She was a nurse back when I visited the halfway house. This mate made a few calls and got me a number. She's still in Sydney in a houso. I rang Sandra and we had a coffee. She let me record this when I said I needed you to hear it.'

Cal sipped from her water caddy and leaned forward.

Dif ran his fingers through his quiff then pressed the play button on his phone screen.

The woman's voice had a burr of croakiness though her tone wasn't without vitality. Just someone older than the pair listening.

"Oh, yeh. We were expecting her. As much as anyone tied down any sort of movement between places to a specific day and time. I mean, if someone didn't turn up it wasn't a biggie. Like oh, must've changed their mind or stayed on at the last place or got more work elsewhere or whatever. And a lot of those women were a bit messy y'know. Stuff they'd been through. Like, you don't end up in some bush-block by accident. I'm not saying that as a judgement. I get it. But some of them were a bit haywire, a bit flighty. Then you add drugs to the mix. Like I said, I don't blame them, the backgrounds some of them came from. But it wasn't a big deal if someone wasn't where they said they were gonna be.

"Thing is I only remember this because we turned another couple of women away by keeping that room free. I felt bad afterwards because they slept in their car down Ultimo and got ripped-off. I'd offered them the couch or the floor but said this other woman, Britta was due to stay. They didn't want to chance it and miss out on other options. So they left. They got done over and Britta never showed. Not everyone had mobis then. It wasn't universal online digital life. Especially feral chicks who were on the move and out bush."

Dif stopped the recording.

'Far out.' Cal shook her head.

'Even I think it's spooky, Cal. She never showed. Not late. Not ever.'

'Yeh and you're not an alarmist drama queen like me. We've got three mentions of a woman called Britta in the right time-frame. All totally independent sources. It's got to be her.'

'It's not irrefutable quite is it? I mean she could have changed her plans and not let on. But still that doesn't seem so likely. She just dropped off the radar.'

'She did. And the fact she didn't turn up in Sydney to the place where she was expected and, as far as we know, she didn't have other contacts there. This casts a rather grim light on her last sighting in Three Rivers.'

Cal gazed into space slowly shaking her head.

***

Next morning Cal was on her way out the back to her work truck in the alley. She could hear Dif in the workshop and went inside.

He was working on the next project, the sleeper. The roadster had already been moved under cover of the lean-to adjoining the workshop.

Dif had just cut the spot-welds from the old frame and was nudging the central door-strut out by tapping it gently with a hammer.

'Bro what's doin? You're up early,' Cal spoke loudly.

Dif pulled back his ear protectors.

'Couldn't sleep. I've had this in my head for days. Thinking of making it a 2-door instead of four.'

'I thought we were doing a sleeper. Isn't that just gonna bring attention?'

'Hm. Maybe.' Dif picked up another door propped against the wall. Lifted it into the space, hooking it onto the hinge mounts. Stood back.

'Man, I'm geeking out on that flow. Imagine if we drop the roofline.'

'Dif. It's a sleeper!' Cal was apoplectic.

'Chill bro. Check it out. Don't you think that looks cool?'

Cal shook her head, moved back a half dozen paces.

'It looks sweet. Too sweet. It won't be under the radar.'

'I know. I just had to see it.'

'It is cool though. You seriously gonna chop the roof?'

'Tempted.' Dif kept staring over the car outline.

'I see it too. Bye bye sleeper.'

Dif picked up a Sharpie pen and angle grinder.

'Bye bye sleeper.'

'Hey before you fire up. I'm sussing a lead on another possible project. I might need a hand getting it though. It's out Kurrajong way. You keen?'

'Count me in. You going to stow it on the farm? Not a lot of space here.'

'That's the plan. Just need to get the okay from Dee.'

She'd need to finish that silo conversion for an AirBnB she'd promised Dee. And keep the new project out of site behind the shearers quarters until she could move it into town. Busy busy.

Cal went to the truck, fired it up. Plugged her phone into the charger. Checked her notifications. Email from Shauna Rojas. She opened it immediately. Several image attachments. She downloaded them and opened them. One at the Wanderground, presumably. Dense bush behind an open grass slope. A young woman in torn denim shorts and a yellow singlet, one hand on the mane of a huge chestnut mare behind her. The woman's hair mid- length with long strands on her shoulders braided with coloured cotton and beads. Britta Kuiper.

The second photo obviously taken on a beach nearing sunset. A group of women around a campfire with a couple of small tents in the background. One in the left foreground with the same woman's face sticking out of the tent-flap, posing with her inverted hands under her chin like a starlet headshot for the camera. Britta. You couldn't miss the tent. A flowered waterproofing fly over the tent with big, stylised daisies in greens and faded white. Cal had never seen one like it. Maybe it was European. Maybe Britta had brought it with her. Could be she had it with her when she visited The Hawkesbury.

Chapter 31

Cal phoned Tyra.

'You gotta n'other book club planned anytime soon?'

'We're always up for an impromptu wine-tasting. What's the go?'

'Got hold of some old photos. Keen for your team to have a squizz. Whaddaya reckon?'

'Let me get back to you.'

Tyra left a voice message that afternoon.

"All set for book club. Charlie's Thurs 7pm."

While Charlie ferried drinks and nibbles to the bench dividing the kitchen from the living room, Tyra introduced a woman Cal hadn't met at the previous get-together. Slightly built and freckled she was a little younger than the other women present.

'Jess, this is Cal.'

'Nice to meet you, Jess.'

'She's another local. Might be able to help,' Tyra said as she directed Cal to the table where Lola sat with a cup of tea.

'The more the merrier,' Cal said.

'Just another book nerd.' Jess smiled.

'I thought this crew were wine buffs. Didn't they tell you?'

'Tea?' Charlie asked, giving Cal the arched eyebrows.

'Great. Thanks.' Cal sat and put her tote beside her on the floor, then withdrew an envelope. She explained about the communal land up north, the Wanderground.

'I managed to get these from a contact up that way. Bless 'er. She knows most of the women who ever stayed at the Wanderground because she was there herself over an eight-year period. And she's kept a lot of old photos. But this is the one I'm most interested in.' Cal slid it onto the table facing Tyra, Charlie, Jess and Lola. The image was yellowed and faded. But you could make out a horseshoe of small tents and a central fireplace. Outside the front of several of the tents pairs and trios of cross-legged women laughing and passing a joint, arms around shoulders.

Lola peered at the photos.

'Oh yeah. She looks vaguely familiar. That's the one I told you about Cal.' Lola tapped a fingernail on one of the figures. 'The woman I saw at the shop that time. Look at the hippie clothes.' She chuckled.

The other women looked at Lola.

'Talked to Cal about it the other day. Remembered this out-of-town woman with a weird accent outside the store. Only saw her that one time. I was helping mum out.'

'Wow, Lola,' Tyra said, incredulous.

'Well it's odd what you think of once you let things drift up from the old memory banks, huh.' Lola raised her eyebrows.

Cal spoke.

'This was taken on the coast up north the month before Britta Kuiper came to Three Rivers. She was staying at The Wanderground and traveled with a group of other women for a full-moon party at the beach. They were big on that kinda thing back then, drumming and howling at the moon or whatevs.' She shrugged, suddenly uncomfortable at her dismissive comment. 'They all camped overnight.' She put her index finger on one of the tents in the background. It had flowers patterned on it. 'This tent-fly was Britta's. It was unique. Same one she would've had here in Three Rivers, presumably.'

Jess spoke first. 'So old-fashioned. You'd wouldn't forget seeing that, would you. Not ringing any bells, though. I don't really remember seeing anyone camping round Three Rivers.'

'It wasn't a thing then so much,' Charlie concurred as she moved a bowl of nuts on the table. Cal noticed a tremor in Charlie's hand.

Lola shook her head. 'Same. I don't remember seeing anything like that. Like you, Jess, I just don't remember people actually camping out here down on the flat . Only locals occasionally but that was in the bush. Not the village. I guess it's the only viable spot though. Everything else is bush or private land.'

Tyra shook her head. 'Sorry, Cal. Before my time. I could ask Pedro though. He might remember something.'

Cal frowned. She felt deflated, frustrated. Her usual response to which was to kick-it-in-the-guts. Why change now?

'So you all kinda socialise together and you all know each other pretty well. Any of the blokes out here seem a bit off?'

'Hey, c'mon,' Tyra, not impressed.

'Well it seems obvious it must've been a local. There's nothing to suggest a young woman came here and met another stranger here and then she never left. No one's ever mentioned a bloke and a chick being here together then leaving separately. If a dodgy bloke wasn't from here then surely he'd dump a body out bush.'

'Don't you think the Lyrebird Track is out bush?' Jess said.

'Everything's relative. My work region is probably more vast and remote than most. I guess I see your point but for a local I reckon that area is still local.'

'It's not very nice looking at your neighbours and thinking the worst. It's like giving into the most base prejudices and suspicions. Applying awful doubts and uncertainties for no good purpose.' Jess's eyes went to the others as she spoke. She wouldn't look directly at Cal who wasn't about to back-peddle any.

Charlie got up and went to the kitchen bench. Jess noticed Charlie's hair was knotty and caught in the hasp of a necklace at the back of her neck.

'Well the purpose is finding a killer. It's not pleasant but it's not exactly a minor problem we're trying to solve. It's ugly,' Cal said irritably. Then it occurred to her then that she might be alone with this. *Small communities stick together*. She was an interloper. These women weren't going to turn on their own menfolk. Even if one of them might be a murderer. Sure, they wanted to help. But they all individually had their own bounds of where they wouldn't look too closely.

Fine. She didn't have to live there. She didn't have to face those people daily. She would ask the nasty questions and hopefully get some answers before everyone clammed up on her.

Jess Barson had been observing the others and feeling the temperature of the room. Though it was her first time there she felt strongly enough about something to speak.

'Um, I've always found that guy at the pub a bit unsavoury.'

No one spoke for a moment.

'Mitch? The barman?' This from Charlie.

Jess' voice quiet as she spoke.

'He calls women from out of town "fresh meat." It's so demeaning. I've heard him say that to other men.'

'It's just the way some men speak,' Tyra said then felt the need to hedge when no one concurred, 'Okay it's not very nice but I don't think they mean anything by it. Anyway his son Troy runs the bar now.'

Cal felt her throat constricting. She was clamping her teeth so tightly her jaw ached. How much did she want to alienate these women? Well, how useful was any information coming out of minds with those attitudes? *Fuck it Nyx you're on your own.*

She coughed and cleared her throat. 'Just gonna use the bathroom,' Cal excused herself.

In the bathroom she leaned against the vanity top her arms rigid and her palms flat. Her eyes were closed as she dropped her head down and breathed out slowly. She lifted her head. The mirror in front of her reflected a cupboard door behind her, slightly ajar. On one of the shelves a wineglass. Cal turned and stepped over to the linen cupboard and gently pulled the door-edge. Piles of clothes looked as though they'd been kicked under the lowest shelf, clumped, preventing the door from closing. The wineglass was a third full.

Well, it was a semi-impromptu meet-up Cal told herself. No time for tidying away. Still, a wineglass in the bathroom. *Whatevs.*

Cal returned to the living room and stood beside the kitchen divider.

'I don't get it. Britta came here. She was used to camping. Someone must have seen her.'

'How do you know she was here?'

It was Jess who'd spoken.

'Well. I guess it's anecdotal. But she was coming here before going on to Sydney. And Lola thinks she saw her,' Cal said.

'I'm pretty sure that's her in the photo. And she said her name was Britta.'

'Maybe she never came. I mean, if no one actually saw her. Maybe she simply changed her plans,' Tyra joined in.

'But I saw her.'

Lola's voice was quiet, as if she might be doubting what she'd said previously.

Like a contagion, Cal wavered with uncertainty, questioned herself.

She'd become fixated on the idea Britta Kuiper came to Three Rivers. But perhaps she really was never there at all. Cal wanted to believe the connection between a young woman traveler at the Wanderground and the mysterious body she found in the freezer. She wanted the story tied up.

A glass smashed in the kitchen.

Cal turned.

Charlie was holding a tea-towel. Flapped it beside her thigh.

'Sorry girls. Clumsy.' Her tongue sounded thick and slurry on the "s" sounds.

Lola stood from the sofa.

'Let me help you with the clean-up, Charlie. Then I've gotta get a move on.'

Tyra and Jess stood as well. Charlie shooed them away from the kitchen.

Cal shrugged a little sheepishly.

'Thanks for gathering y'all. I really appreciate your interest. Maybe I've been a bit single-minded and blinkered. Hope I haven't wasted your time.'

She thanked Charlie and moved to the front door. The other friends said their goodbyes and dispersed.

Outside, as she sat in her truck, Cal brewed over what had been said. Which wasn't a lot and maybe that was part of her dissatisfaction. She started her truck then reversed and turned. As she did so she glimpsed what looked like a single-lane bridge through the shrubbery. She'd not noticed it before, always concentrating on the downstream view. It ran across the stream from what looked like the boundary of Charlie's property.

Cal exited Charlie's driveway. Despite her misgivings, and the creeping doubt that she'd possibly led herself along an obscure and wayward theory, there was still a part of her that gripped a shred of her first premise. She couldn't quite let go of it.

Yeh, okay, so none of these women tonight had seen Britta and that tent. But Lola reckons she'd seen her at the store. A one-off. What about the men? What if Britta had arrived late in the day towards the evening? Even if she'd arrived earlier and explored around for somewhere to camp or followed the road out to the old cemetery she'd want a place to camp before dark. The pub would've been the only place still open, above the only likely camping spot. Did any of the men in the pub see her? Cal needed to inspect the area again. Tomorrow morning she promised herself.

She remembered something else she'd been meaning to follow up. She wrote a quick email to both Sierra Gambel and to Shauna Rojas, the two women who'd been with Britta at the Wanderground. She asked them, without being specific, if they remembered Britta wearing any distinctive jewellery. Then she fired up the truck and headed for home.

Chapter 32

CAL DROVE TO THREE Rivers and parked under the trees that ringed the boundary of the Bushman's Rest pub.

She climbed from the cab and stood, scoping the surrounds. Away from the air-conned cocoon of her truck's cab she felt her shirt back collapse against her skin in the steamy air. She reached back inside and grabbed her water canteen taking a long slug before scanning up and down the river.

The view of the watercourse wasn't constant and uninterrupted. To the north the waterway was visible because the land was cleared, prefaced by a grassy bank. Directly in front of where she stood in the carpark the river was unseen because of a tree-covered slope. She walked under the shading trees and along to the south where the bridge crossed the river. The support abutments were high. Following the grass downhill, she wandered under the bridge then turned and looked back. The grassed area swept on a gently rising plateau then ran up a much steeper bank to the plateau where the pub stood. The building wasn't the original pub. That one was swept away in a long-ago flood. It had stood on the lower plateau. The flat expanse that was now the camping area.

She followed the lower sweep back towards the northern point and stood when she was in line with the carpark of the pub. The drop away was significant. She leaned on a wooden picnic table and took another swallow from her water canteen. Had a think. If she'd pitched a small tent down here it wouldn't be visible from up there at the pub or even the carpark, 'cept maybe if someone was on the edge, under the trees up there and actually looking for it.

Cal thought on what had been said back at Charlie's place about the publican. A son was mentioned as well, Troy. Was he the same age as the others? She couldn't recall his name coming up in previous conversations.

As she walked back up the grassy slope to the carpark she stopped on the rim and scanned below her. Difficult to see the area near the picnic table. South towards the bridge was more open to her present sightline.

Cal pushed through the side door of the pub. Inside was dim and the temperature barely cooler than outside. Folks in several small groups and pairs were gathered at tables beside windows along the front and side walls with views beyond the shaded verandas to the river and ranges beyond. Day-trippers Cal surmised. Locals would probably arrive later after work.

She went to the bar where a tall, grizzled man with sallow skin was cracking coin rolls and filling the till slider pockets.

'Do for ya,' he asked without raising his eyes.

'Lime and soda thanks,' Cal replied while eying the Duty Manager board behind the bar. The name tag in the slot: Mitch Medenhall. Maybe son Troy would be working later.

Medenhall screwed up the coin wrappers and tossed them somewhere under the bar.

'Lime's cordial. Not fresh.'

'All good,' Cal said. Her stomach made an audible angst of hunger.

'You do toasties or anything?' she added.

The barman was topping her glass off from the mixer hose. He put her drink in front of her and slid a plastic covered menu along the bar.

'Thanks.'

She scanned quickly.

'Cheese and tomato toastie, thanks.'

'Coming up,' he said then turned and walked further along the back of the bar before poking his head through a wooden hatch and speaking to someone in the kitchen.

Cal sipped her drink. It tasted like coca cola.

A nineties soundtrack was playing quietly through speakers, Oasis, 'Champagne Supernova.'

Ten minutes later a flush-faced, heavyset woman in an apron delivered her sandwich. Medenhall was beside the till looking at a tablet screen occasionally scrolling with his thumb. Cal ate her sandwich.

'Mind if I ask you a few questions,' she said when she'd finished.

He looked at her and raised his eyebrows, lips pressed together.

'You owned this place a long time? Like back in the late eighties, early nineties.'

'Been here all my life.'

'So, you were the publican back then?'

'Yep.'

'Never left here or worked anywhere else?'

'Nup,' he said.

She found that hard to imagine but remained impassive.

He spoke again, 'What's it to ya?'

'I found that body on the ridge.'

'Ah.' It was a short exclamation. 'Bit of a shocker.' He looked at her uniform and Ranger patches. 'You're not a copper.'

'No. Did anyone else tend bar back then? You must've needed a break sometimes?'

'The wife and I both did shifts but mostly me. Then she pissed off so it was just me.'

'Do you remember a girl staying here that autumn?'

'Ya kidding, right?' He planted both palms on the bar.

'Well, she had a distinctive tent-fly with flowers on it and she was Dutch. Spoke with quite an accent. She was camped just below here on the flats by the river.'

'Gimme a break,' Medenhall scoffed.

Cal tried another tack. 'You've got a son, yeh? He grew up here?'

Medenhall cocked an eyebrow. 'No he didn't. Missus wanted him to have a city education. So much for her thinking. He ended up back here anyway.'

'Oh well. Maybe he appreciated the broader view an education elsewhere might have afforded.' Cal's smile resembled a grimace.

'You're free with your opinions aren't ya?' Medenhall's eyes were cast over the top of Cal's head. His eyebrows raised in acknowledgement of someone she couldn't see. Then she used the mirror that backed the bottle shelves behind the bar and saw the woman who was somewhat familiar but she couldn't place her. She was walking to the bathrooms adjacent to a side entrance.

'Just trying to get a feel for the place. Piece together what might have happened to that girl.'

Medenhall grunted then busied himself at the far end of the bar then disappeared beyond the kitchen down a short hallway.

Cal took another sip of her strangely flavoured beverage and was reminded why it was still three quarters full. She turned on her stool and stared across the room through the windows to the outdoor area and beyond. She took a deep breath and let it out slowly then pushed her stool back from the bar and left a twenty dollar note under her glass.

She scuffed outside and over to her truck trying to conjure a possible scene there more than two decades prior. Attractive young woman. Not a local. The publican with a reputation as a womaniser and misogynist. Or had Medenhall's son Troy tried it on with Britta Kuiper? He can't have been away all the time. What about school holidays? Maybe he stayed with his mother. She remembered the photos Charlie had shown her. Medenhall junior was a contemporary of that friend group. Medenhall senior was rangy. His son was too going by those photos. She sighed with frustration. *Yeh, or any other bloke in the pub that night. Or some bloke who wasn't at the pub.*

Desperation, Cal. You've got nothing. She ran over it all again. No one seemed to know if Britta Kuiper was around there camping in a tent or where else she might have stayed. No one had come forward to say she stayed with them, then or now. She must have camped. Unless she did stay with someone. And that person did away with her.

Chapter 33

SHE'D SEEN THE THING peeping from a half-collapsed lean-to shed in a paddock that bordered a private Parks Service road. She was scoping a ridge through her field glasses when she discovered it, having dropped her view back down to ground level to confirm her bearings. If the shed had been closer to a public road some other eagle-eyed fanatic would have commandeered the vehicle long ago. Cal noted the position and figured how to access the farm it was attached to once she'd finished work.

Later that day, she'd approached the elderly owner and made an offer then organised Dif to come out to Kurrajong on a train to help her retrieve it.

Cal picked him up at the station and with a couple of hours of daylight left.

Dif climbed in after dropping a backpack full of tools into the rear of the cab.

'Remind me from here on in that I'm not a fan of public transport.'

'Just a one-off mate. You need a debrief?'

'No thanks. Just distract me with why I'm here.'

'Mate I couldn't leave it for someone else. Had to grab it. Carpe diem an' all that.'

They unearthed the EK Holden and tinkered and cajoled it into firing up. Caked in decades of dust and bird droppings it didn't look promising. But Cal was convinced the bodywork, kept from the elements for so long, would clean up to presentable status.

'We can't drive this thing legally on the road. It's basically a wreck,' Dif said.

'Patina mate. It's a thing. We'll be under the radar.' Cal soothed, running her hand over the surface rust.

'We don't have brakes. It's a deathtrap.'

'They're a bit spongy, granted. I'll just save them for emergencies. Still got the hand-brake. Chill. Look we'll wait for dark. Only gotta get it to Dee's place. Have a wee campfire in the meantime. We'll be sweet. C'mon. Help me collect some firewood.'

'What about redbacks and scorpions?'

'Thought you were a hippie at some point'

'One with limitations and boundaries.'

'God's sake bro. Nothin here to hurt you. You really need to get out of the city more.'

'Might be right.'

Cal went to her truck and retrieved something from a toolbox. Tossed it at Dif.

'Here's some gloves. Feel better now?'

'I didn't used to be wimpy. What's happened to me?'

'Too much online life.'

'I barely do online.'

'You're right. There's no excuse then. You're doomed.' Cal had an empty twenty litre paint bucket in her hand. She began tossing in small chunks of hardwood from the surrounds.

'Need bigger bits than that won't we?' Dif whined.

'Hardwood knots. That's why they haven't rotted. This is the hot stuff.'

'I'll gather some kindling then.'

They both scuffed about collecting material and dumping it beside a hollow and rocks Cal had formed into a firepit.

'Got some brewskis in that esky on the tray. Wanna grab 'em?'

She busied herself setting the fire while Dif went back to the truck, lifted the lid on the cooler and grabbed two bottles.

When Cal had a decent blaze going she did another quick sweep beyond and returned with a near full bucket. Tossed a few more pieces on the fire. Plumes of embers bowed skywards as the pieces landed then settled in the flames. She tipped the remaining stash on the ground and offered the upturned bucket to Dif.

'Nah I'm good. More comfy on my haunches thanks mate.'

She took the bucket seat.

Dif flicked the cap from a bottle with a screwdriver and passed it to Cal.

'Cheers, queers.' They clinked bottles. Sat and stared at the blaze. Cal stretched her neck and gazed into the darkness.

'Lookit that sky.'

'So awesome. I miss seeing it like this in the city,' Dif replied.

A nightjar called from the darkness.

'The stars are burnt out suns or some-such, right?' Cal said.

'They're like little nuclear reactors, burning up gas. Even the sun's a star.'

'A very big star then. Doesn't it make your head hurt thinking about the universe?'

Dif chuckled. 'Haven't really thought about it that way. But it's awesome for sure.'

'The universe, infinity, it's so huge,' Cal sighed. 'And it's uninhabitable. Space goes forever and this little blue planet is the only one that supports life. And we're here. By some accident of mixed DNA and shit we exist in this whole universe. What are the chances? Makes my brain implode. I can't get my head around it.'

'It's pretty spooky. Yeh.'

They drank a few beers as darkness enveloped the surrounds. Let the fire die down.

'Whaddaya reckon mate? Let's get the beastie home.'

'Okey dokes.' Dif stood and stretched. They toed sand over the embers and wandered back to the Holden.

Cal fiddled with a rubber hose from under the bonnet then sat inside and wiggled a screwdriver in the ignition switch, firing the machine up.

'Yii haaa.'

'You want me to nurse a petrol can in my lap with a hose running through the firewall to the carb?' Dif asked.

'It'll work. Think of it as an adventure. You love it. C'mon it's like the old days.'

'You're insane.'

'Okay. Just close your eyes then. And keep that thing upright bro. Actually, before you close your peepers we need a GPS route through the back roads. Either that or check my topo maps. Nah, you're gonna have your eyes shut. Best we go with the GPS.'

'There's intermittent signal out here at best.'

'You're right. Maybe I should just follow my nose.'

'Seriously Cal you're off the charts.'

'Well we have to do something. C'mon. Indulge me. Look the smoke's clearing.'

Cal revved the engine and wiped the side mirror with the elbow of her hoodie as she looked towards the exhaust pipe at the rear.

'She's rarin' to go. We'll be sweet.'

Dif shook his head and steadied the gas-can between his knees.

'Tally-ho.' He punched the air with a clenched fist.

'Now ya talkin'.'

Cal eased the shifter into first gear and gently raised the clutch pedal. The machine crawled forward bouncing and squeaking.

'Suspension's shot,' she said.

'No surprise there.'

Then an unholy metallic shriek came from the rear in rhythmic waves.

'Jesus what's that?' Cal winced.

'Brake drums probably seized with corrosion. Hope they don't snap the springs before they loosen off,' Dif grimaced.

Cal moved through the gears.

'Hope they make their mind up soon. That noise is painful.'

'Best you fang it then.'

'Yeh, when in doubt, add more throttle.'

She floored it. The rear end chomped into the gravel and the front end lifted. She loosened her grip on the wheel, grinned, pushed herself back into the sagging seat.

Chapter 34

SOMETHING HAD UNSETTLED JESSICA Barson. Something was irritating her unconscious like a piece of remnant rose thorn stuck under calloused skin. The presence apparent but the pain no longer acute. A reminder, an infinitesimal shifting somewhere deep in her memory.

What had she done and where had she been in the last little while? What had triggered this dislodged sense?

She drank her coffee as she watched a pair of ducks emerge from the rushes on the pond margins. They swept their beaks through the grass then both birds sat, tucking their legs away, necks dropped down into their chests.

Her window was open. A light rain fell, misty edges on the dark water. Jessica scratched absently at the side of her left knee, the cool air from the open window chilling the old wound, the scar tissue ache around the joint. She pulled the window until only an inch was open and rubbed her hand over her knee to warm it, then stopped.

Her knee. The old wound. A bike accident on her grandfather's birthday, his last one ever. A week later he was gone.

***

She's riding her bike on the quiet river road early
one Sunday morning. She always rides like her mum
told her, keeping left, not leaving anything to chance
when some driver might come the other way too far
over on the unmarked gravel surface. A water dragon
emerges up ahead from the dusty margins of scrub.
It stops when it sees her, rises high on its rear legs.
Jessica brakes and yanks on her handlebars to change
the trajectory. Her front wheel washes out in the deep
gravel at the roadside and falls. Her body keeps going,
airborne, then not. Her left knee takes the brunt of her
momentum when a broken slab of shale gashes open
the flesh around her kneecap. The force of her weight
and speed gouging into the cartilage and bone as her
kneecap goes sideways.

The water dragon scuttles across the road, its hind
legs rotating like off-kilter chopper blades. Jessica clasps
her mangled joint. It's bleeding, not heavily but the
damage is evident. A burning ache stabs deep and sharp
within the joint. She moans rocking back and forth as
she holds tightly, both hands around the wound. Her
bike fallen in the gravel and weeds at the roadside.

Who might come by to help? She's in the middle
of nowhere on a Sunday morning. Hikers? Tourists?
People making their way to church? The swimming
hole at Three Rivers?

She can't ride or even walk. She needs a crutch. Maybe she can crawl into the scrub and find something to lean on. A branch that might do the job. But first pull the bike onto the road edge. Make sure someone will have to stop. She needs help.

She drags herself into a sitting position and rests on her elbows. Letting go of her leg makes the pain seem worse. She clutches at the wound again squeezing her fingers tight. This won't do. C'mon Jess, you can't just lie here. If she has to drag her leg with her jeans torn open, she'll get dirt and stuff in there. Should wrap it up. Might help with the bleeding too. She lets go of her knee. Ignores the surge of pain and wriggles out of her lightweight jacket. She winds the arms of the garment under and around the middle of her leg and pulls the cuffs tight to begin a knot. Not enough length but a half-knot will have to do.

She turns her body so her head and torso face down towards the scrub, figuring she'll have to drag her messed-up leg face-up behind her to avoid contact with the rough ground. Sharp rocks and spiky dried-out weed stalks dig into her palms and wrists as she pulls her body backwards, her good leg scrabbling and pushing her through the uncomfortable surrounds. Her progress is sluggish but negotiating the terrain seems to distract her from the ache of her leg. The road faces north and the sun shines directly onto her face and body through the swathe cut in the forest trees by the roadway. The heat doesn't help.

As she works her way closer to the taller scrub where she hopes to find a suitable branch, the way becomes harder, the vegetation thicker and more tangled. This isn't going to be easy at ground level. As she pauses and contemplates her options she hears the engine whine of an approaching vehicle. She turns and rolls her body, gasping as her mangled knee now forced to rotate, rasps across the rubble and debris. She claws at the ground calling for help. Pressing her good foot for purchase she stretches her neck as the engine noise gets closer and she pushes and drags her body to the road edge.

'Help me. Please help me.' She cries out as she raises her body as high as she can manage. The vehicle is visible now, an old green Land Rover, and it's slowing down. Jessica begins to cry as she sees the driver pull onto the verge. He gets out and rushes to her side.

Her head drops in relief as she sobs.

'Poor girl. Let me help you.' He says, kneeling at her side.

Chapter 35

Two weeks prior. The noise woke Charlie. The beauty of a tin roof. Scarily raucous at times like this though. Not a sonorous lullaby pitter-pat. More a steel ball hammering like truckloads of gravel sheeting down from a precipitous altitude.

She hurried to the window and drew open the wooden blinds. Could barely see to midway across the yard as curtains of cascading rain fell in grey veils. The stream would've breached the banks for certain. House and foundation piers should be okay though. They'd survived floods before. Still, best check the yards when this lot abated. Couldn't be far off now she hoped as she went to the kitchen to make tea.

She angled a high stool at the bench and drank as she watched and listened. The clamour began to lose its intensity.

After twenty minutes the sound of the water dripping from the eaves into puddles below accompanied the reappearance of her yards. She rinsed her teacup and pulled on her gumboots draping a Drizabone coat over her shoulders. The ground outside wasn't exactly spongy, not enough clay in it for that, but it was waterlogged and puddled. The deluge hadn't percolated down through the layers. Likely the subterranean layers were also full and the surface was the only escape. She sloshed carefully across the yard towards the banks of the stream. A murky torrent sailed past, frothy in patches with random logs and debris. She kept her distance, caution necessary due to the velocity of the passing water. Despite the lull in the downpour, more water would be making its way down from the hills to swell the watercourse even further.

A lump of stream bank clumped with grass fell away as she stood and watched. Its hold on the ground undercut by the overnight torrent. She followed the trajectory of the chunk as it slowly sank lower and dragged forward with the current. Her eyes scanned the margins of the waterway then settled on the right-angled, pristine white corners of a square object exposed further along her yard. *Oh. Weird.*

Maintaining her distance from the water's edge she moved towards the object. Her gumboots threatened to pull off her feet. Closer now the object looked like an old freezer and it didn't look as though it had floated there. It seemed embedded but now uncovered by the water wash and erosion on one side.

She'd lived there all her life. She didn't remember ever seeing a freezer in the yard. Her parents wouldn't have dumped it there. They always disposed of their junk at the refuse station. And anyway it didn't have the rounded edges of those really old-style contraptions. So its presence seemed more contemporary. But only she lived there. More to clean-up when this lot dries out, she thought.

Despite the rain having stopped Charlie Stone gave the surrounds the rest of the day and following evening to settle and drain fully.

The sun was out next morning and a slight westerly breeze was a welcome aid to the drying out required. Her back lawn was silted and beached waves of fine debris marked the stages of the receding water-level.

Charlie collected a rake and spade from her garden tool shed and made her way to the white freezer protruding like a broken tooth from a gum. Such a random problem. How the hell was she going to move the thing?

Chapter 36

Cal was running another theory past Scobie.

'Despite it being long before social media and the internet there seemed to be this under-ground knowledge of this place. Internationally, I mean. There were women coming here from all over Europe, the States, everywhere. Word just got around these disparate women's communities that there was land owned by women where only women were welcome. Where they could be safe. Can you imagine knowing that? With the background of violence so many of us come from. You'd move heaven and earth to visit, wouldn't you? Just to know what it felt like not having to look over your shoulder all the time, to be free of that. I mean I don't believe in some kind of hippie, rural utopia. But I totally get the appeal of shedding hyper-vigilance for a time. According to Shauna Rojas, spoke to her the other day,' she clarified, 'this girl Britta was estranged from her family and she was making her way down the eastern seaboard.'

'So you think this woman, a backpacker, might be the Jane Doe?'

'Why not? The thing that always gets me is that she was never reported missing. How could that happen? It could only be someone who had no family or was estranged from family or lost from family. Isn't a woman who has traveled from the other side of the planet to get away from an abusive, religious family the perfect victim? If her family disowned her and ceased to acknowledge her they never would have tried to find out where she'd gone. Surely we could check Customs and Immigration records from around that time and see if she ever left the country. Cos if she didn't leave and she'd disappeared from all other records here then where the hell is she? Short of leaving here on a boat.'

'Well, that's always a possibility too. But as you say it's pretty straightforward to check if she left via usual means. You know, it's also feasible she didn't want to be found. Maybe she changed her name? She could be alive and well living her life free of a past she wanted to forget.'

'I think it needs checking out. She was on her way to Sydney. She never got there. There's a connection to her and the Hawkesbury at the right time. We can't ignore it.'

'Yes, I agree. It's quite compelling.'

'You're quite compelling.' Cal curled her fingers around the back of Scobie's neck and pulled her close.

'You're a nut.' Scobie laughed, her head dropping back, neck exposed.

***

Cal did her own research hoping she might clarify or trip over something useful by following the tracks that Britta Kuiper could have taken. She knew from her own time spent in the local cemeteries that the earliest graves were mostly men. But Britta had been looking for a female relative. How far back had Britta been looking?

There were definitely Dutch present from the early days of the white invasion in 1788. A few sailors and explorers, even convicts shipped from Britain, who'd been born in the Netherlands. That surprised Cal. The laptop was getting hot on her thighs. The gaffer tape holding the back on got wiggly as the adhesive melted. *Bodgy as. N'other job for Pirate.* Back to her research. There were Dutch growers in the London region in the sixteen hundreds. The city was expanding fast and struggling to produce enough food and the Dutch were canny. They knew how to create hotbeds and use manure to get bountiful yields from their crops. It seemed plausible to Cal that the Dutch presence in the Hawkesbury might have devolved from the London mob. Perhaps some who'd fallen foul of the law had been deported to Australia. They were certainly present in colonial agriculture and horticulture from the eighteen hundreds in that area. Another possibility was that the Dutch in the region came via the gold-diggers a little later or mariners jumping ship in the eighteen fifties gold-rush. Unlikely that would've been a woman though.

Then there were settlers. *The land grabs.* Cal squirmed then re-focussed.

Turns out, all but one of the Dutch settlers in the Hawkesbury region was male. Far out. That narrows things down. Must've made Britta's job easier. Mine too.

Also, how the hell would you survive then if you were the only woman, the only white woman in the region? She would've stuck out. She would've been some kind of target. Men would've latched on to her. What if she was a grower? What if she wanted to maintain her independence? Did she pretend she was a man? *Not unheard of for sure. Risky.*

Or maybe she was a grower, yes, but a widow. She'd worked with her husband, learnt from her family and him, but he died. Again, she wanted to maintain her independence, supply the expanding community. Legitimate. Support herself and not need to remarry. *Possible.*

Was this the relative Britta was looking for?

Later, when she was talking again to Scobie. 'Well, there were a few women around then. Not many though. Those early arrivals, apart from the convicts who were both men and women, but the settlers who came later, they were predominantly men. I guess that's why they targeted indigenous women.' She grimaced.

'Sadly for them.'

'Yup.' Cal breathed out slowly.

'I was thinking, what if a woman was widowed. They'd be onto her like a rash. What if she didn't want a bloke hanging around? What if she had her own means of support? Would she move away and dress as a male to protect herself?'

'Hmm,' Scobie murmured, 'So you're suggesting that our young woman was here looking for an ancestor. That's why she was in this area?'

'Makes sense to me. And two women from the Wanderground have confirmed it. Also tidies up why she was only here a short time. She was due in Sydney. This was a quick side-track. She was doing something that was important to her. She'd come from the other side of the world.'

'Well, it's a scenario, I guess. How on earth are you going to firm that up?'

'Throw me a bone, Scobes. Aren't you always going on about keeping an open mind? What have your lot come up with?'

'Can always rely on you for a realistic appraisal. Touchy bugger. We have hundreds of leads that need to be followed up, you realise. Not something that gets cleared quickly. You're right though. No point limiting ourselves. I tip my hat to you once again, Nyx. And all power to you coming up with the goods to support that theory. We all want the same outcome, right?'

'Right.'

'Petulant sod.'

'Right.'

Cal gnawed on a loose thread hanging from her shirt cuff.

'Identifying the victim is a fairly crucial step, isn't it?'

'Absolutely. No where to go without that,' Scobie replied.

'And we might be at that juncture. I've given you a name.'

'Could be close, yes.'

'I know you're dying to thank me.'

Then Cal shook herself into a more serious mode.

'Hey, any news on your step-dad?'

Scobie looked up. She compressed her lips and puffed a little air from her handsome nose. Blinked.

'Thanks for asking. He's home now. I think he may need some rehab and I can't imagine that's going to go down well. I'll visit when things settle here, assuming he remains on the mend.'

Cal nodded.

'Nice one, Scobes.'

Chapter 37

ONE WEEK PRIOR. THE freezer discovery and police statement are televised on Channel Nine Evening News.

'What the...'

'No. No no no. Can't be,' he mutters alone in the room. Then he stands one hand clutching his stomach.

Calm down. Must be someone else's freezer. With a body in it.

The stupidity of this thought strikes him.

The Lyrebird Track. They could be naming the dark face of the moon; such is the specificity of this remote and barren stretch.

"A padlocked lid."

How's that for a distinguishing feature? But I never padlocked it. Weird. Still think you might be off the hook?

He drops to his knees.

Not reported to police. Dumped. Spotted by some park ranger. Dumped?

Soooo, whoever shot it over that cliff edge they knew what was in it? But if they knew what was in it why didn't they call the police? Doesn't make sense. And who could've found it? It was buried. Private property. The property owner? Has *she sold? No, I'd have known that. Got a Google alert on the address. So, <u>she</u> found it. Her. Why not go to the cops?*

Is she scared of me? But she doesn't know it's me. Or has she figured something out?

She's going to try and blackmail me. Is that it?

Cops all over the place speaking to everyone. She'll crack for sure. Nope. Can't take the risk.

She needs to be dealt with.

***

Cal made a follow up call to Scobie.

'You questioned all the locals, right?'

'Standard procedure, yes.'

'No one missed out?'

'Not to my knowledge.'

'And it came out that this young woman left the area. Intact. She was alive. She got a lift out of town.'

'Mm hmm. I see where this is going Cal. Last person to see her alive.'

'He was questioned by police like most of the other locals. He was heading to Windsor that day and offered her a lift to the train station there so she could get to Sydney. And because no one ever reported Britta Kuiper missing and no one ever found the body. There was no suspicion, no case, no investigation. It was an innocent and casual reference to a traveler who had visited the area long ago. No one has ever questioned whether she actually left.'

'Yes. A very important point.'

'Another thing. Who are the neighbours to Charlie Stone's farm?'

Scobie brought up a document on her laptop.

'Duane and Jody Nestor one side, B.C. Kaplan on the other. They're directly adjoining, either side.'

'Have their names come up at all in your investigation?'

'No.'

'Have you got a map there?'

While Scobie opened another document finger-spread the image to bring up the relevant region Cal continued.

'I don't get it. I've been to Charlie's place. There's a bridge there across the Langdon Stream. It must be a private access-way.'

'Relevance?' Scobie said.

'Well that's a neighbour. Across the river with a private access between. Still a neighbour. Also more private than the neighbour's with an adjoining road access, if you get me. And I saw diggings at Charlie's place by the stream. Can we do a property search and see who owns it?'

'Give me a minute.' Scobie went to a database via a password.

'Owners names, Ella and Reed Ballard.'

Never heard of them. Cal slumped at her end of the call.

'Pfftt. Does it give a purchase date?'

'Last sale was April 2009.'

'Previous owners?'

'Negative. Only dates. No names.'

'Dammit.' Cal pulled at her lower lip. Then her phone pinged with email notifications.

'Hang on a tick. Need to check these.'

Cal opened the emails.

'Wow.'

'What is it?'

'Heard back from both of those women who knew Britta. They've both confirmed she wore copper jewellery. A labrys earring and a snake bracelet that wound up her right wrist.'

'That's pretty persuasive. Can you ask them if they're okay with my team contacting them?'

'Onto it.'

***

Cal rapped on the door at Pirate's Arncliffe address, calling out as she did so.

'Police. Open up.'

Half a minute later Pirate opened the door, held it ajar but wouldn't look at Cal.

'Juvenile.'

'Scobie would probably concur,' Cal said.

'So, the crystals are working, huh?'

'Despite my doubts and lack of buy-in it seems so.'

'Can't beat the cosmic field, my friend.'

'I've always been lucky mate.'

'Aha.' Nodding but unconvinced. 'So, what brings you into this den of wonder? What's today's challenge?'

Pirate muted her speakers and reduced the visual field to her big-screen where the F1 qualifying sessions for the Italian Grand Prix were taking place.

'Hey, keep that on mate. Kiwi driver on his second start there.'

'Yes, they're expecting much from young Liam. He did himself proud on debut.' Pirate brought the full-size screen back up.

'Wet track n'all. Some are likening him to McLaren.'

'Yes. A bit early for comparisons with Bruce, I say.'

'Agreed. Okay, little poser for you.' Cal pinned Pirate with a steady look. 'Can you do a search on this for me?'

She handed Pirate a slip of paper.

Chapter 38

Tambor saw the younger freak leave the Petersham property via the back lane. An involuntary sneer formed at his mouth. His plastered right arm rested on the top of the steering wheel. He refelt the shattering blow that had smashed his wrist.

As the small figure approached the far end of the lane way Tambor quietly left his vehicle and sneaked along the shadowed side of the alley. When close to the entrance of the garage he stopped and waited and listened. There was no work noise from inside. He stepped closer to the open doorway and peered past the vehicle to the workbench at the rear. Light fell across the worktop from a side door in the yard. No one was at the bench.

Tambor scuttled into the garage and hid behind the main door closest to the street. He could see through the hinged gap across to the side door. He waited. Desperate for a smoke.

Ten minutes passed.

He heard the scuffing footsteps as someone approached from the yard. Stangler's stooped form entered the side door, a coffee mug in hand. Stangler put the mug down on the bench and moved to the opposite side where a vice was clamped onto the worktop. He picked up a metal object and placed it in the vice, his right hand tightening the jaw handle. Then he took a long-handled file and began rasping the metal's edge. Tambor moved from his hiding place, an old-fashioned leather-covered sap in his left hand. It felt slightly awkward in his non-dominant fist.

Tambor sidled past the parked vehicle and raised his hand as he approached Stangler.

His left foot collided with something jutting from beneath the car.

Stangler turned. Tambor swung at his head clouting Dif but caught the back of his skull, not the temple. Stangler stumbled and turned, raising his left hand. Tambor caught him with a back-swing right across the side of his head. Dif dropped to the floor.

Tambor moved quickly to the alleyway then forced himself to stroll slowly to where his car was parked. He got in and drove up the alley. He left the car running and and opened the boot. From inside the garage he dragged Stangler along the floor and dropped him beside the rear door. He checked the alley was clear then pulled Stangler to the open boot where he struggled his body inside, hefting him from below with his shoulders and back. He slammed down the boot-lid.

Tambor left Petersham and headed for the Princes Highway and South Coast.

Two hours later he parked in the layby above the surf spot with the view across to the new subdivision. Below the parking area the reef dropped off into deep water. The swells thundered into the rocks below.

The sun had completely dropped behind the looming escarpment in the west. A thin rim of fiery orange backlit the treetops in silhouette before quickly disappearing into twilight. Tambor put a foot up on the low log-wood carpark barrier and lit a fag. Lights dappled the subdivision across the small valley. He puffed and blew smoke with energy like he was ridding his body of something beyond tar and tannins.

He turned back to the car and opened the boot-lid.

Dif squinted at the brightness from the vehicle's courtesy lamps. He was on his back. His arms retracted defensively. A large, bruised lump swelled from his right-side temple.

'Outcha get,' Tambor said taking another drag on his cigarette.

Dif clambered out and stumbled as the numbness in his right leg collapsed his knee.

Tambor nudged him towards the low fence. He lit another cigarette from the last one.

'Ever seen the view from up there? The dumpsite? Great vistas along the coast. Primo. Some clown from Lasprilla's past owned that land. Long, long time ago. Had to sell. Hard luck story. Most of it would've been rural. Still a couple of farms on the other side of the main road. No views there of course. Anyway, this bloke was a son of that family. He always wanted to hold onto the land and get it back someday. In the interim, he'd had some dealing with Lasprilla's family. Did the dirty. I dunno what. But whatever it was, Lasprilla brooded on it for years.'

Dif listened, totally nonplussed. The surrounds however were more than familiar.

Tambor rattled on.

'He was a successful developer and when he got the chance, he bought that land. And then he opened it up as a dumpsite for rock spoil and crap from building sites. Couldn't warrant it could ya, things people do to get even. He developed the land down the bottom near the coast. Then he basically shat on the land that used to belong to this other joker's family. Just to spite him.'

Tambor continued.

'Stupid isn't it. Giving your life-source, your energy over to a slight. Letting your pride fire up something so long cold. Stoking it and blowing air under it.'

The hypocrisy wasn't lost on Dif, who remained silent.

'Still, that's not your problem is it? Your problem is me.'

Chapter 39

Jess Barson sat at the window. What had Cal the ranger asked about at Charlie's the other night? Britta Kuiper, the traveling Dutch girl. The photo she'd shown of a beach camp, Britta up north. Her tent-fly with the olive-green flowers on it.

Why was any of that significant?

Because Jess had finally remembered an incident and a date that pinned it very specifically in time. And as she did so, her finger, presently rubbing back and forth over the scar on her knee, began to tremble and a dark chasm opened beneath her and any sense of grounding or certainty in her surrounds fell away into the blackness.

He slides her bike into the back of the old Land Rover and leans it along the side bench seat. He's visiting his parents' farm on a uni break.

He helps her into the back so she can keep her leg straight along the other bench seat.

On the ride to her home, as she clenches the gory wound between her fingers, she sees something jammed between the opposite bench seat and the rear of the driver's seat. A nylon thing with stylised flowers on it. She notices the flowers. An odd thing for a man to have, girlie, or something a child might like. It can't belong to him surely. Or his parents for that matter.

Chapter 40

Cal got a call from an unknown number. She answered. It was Mitch Medenhall.

'Need to talk to you about something. Can you drop by the pub?'

'Yeh, I can do that. You working tonight?'

'Yup. Here now 'til closing.'

Cal finished work that day and, before going to The Bushman's Rest, she traveled along the Lower Three Rivers Track to check something in the old cemetery. She parked and walked over to the area most recently cleared by the volunteers where she'd taken a break last time she was there. She checked the headstone.

'Sacred to the Memory of Isa Braam
Who departed this life June 5th 1846 aged 71 years'
She left the cemetery and drove to The Bushman's Rest, parked her truck behind the pub and went inside.

It was busier than the last time she'd been there during the day. Most of the tables were occupied by groups of people and the bar counter was crowded as well. Maybe locals and weekenders getting an early start on things.

She went to a gap at the far end of the bar and caught Medenhall's eye. Both he and his son were on duty. The elder came and took Cal's order when the bar crush thinned out. He returned with a bottle of Peroni.

'That night you were talking about. I did see something. I saw that tent. It was near the picnic table.'

Cal looked at him, frowned and shook her head. Her lips parted like she was about to exclaim.

'Why didn't you say something before now?' Her voice grated with frustration and antagonism.

'Couldn't. Tricky situation. Hadn't even thought of it. Then you were poking around and everyone's speculating. People remember stuff. Like your memory wakes up.'

'Really?' Cal didn't hide her incredulity.

'Keep this under your hat, okay. I was seein someone. Longstanding thing after the missus left. Awkward for her 'cos she was still hitched. Still is. Get the picture?'

Cal flicked her eyebrows up in assent.

'We'd meet in front of the CFA hall under the bridge.'

Cal translated in her head. Country Fire Association. Medenhall continued.

'I'd wander down after closing time. Walk along the bank there 'stead of the road. I saw that tent there that night. Didn't think much of it. Not like the locals camped there much. Picnics and bonfires, but not camping over. Still, occasionally travelers camped. More nowadays. But local kids went bush for that. Get away from the olds. Never brought it up cos I'd have needed a good reason for going down there to the river flat in the middle of the night.'

'So who else could've seen it?'

'No one. Unless they did what I did and walked down the bank to keep out of sight. Locals would drive here to the pub or walk home via the roadway. Safer. Better lit. Not so slippery. No reason for anyone going the route I did. And I did it regularly.'

'So, this woman you met. Would she have seen the tent?'

'Nah. CFA is around a bend in the river. She'd wait for me there in her 4x4. She never mentioned it if she did.'

'Mind me asking who you met up with?'

'Rather not. Small town. Too risky.'

'Fair enough. I'd keep schtum though.'

'Nah.'

'Okay. Well thanks for telling me this. It's pretty important info.' She couldn't restrain herself from adding, 'Wish I'd had it before now. You know I've got to pass this onto police. Unless you have already. They're gonna be spewing. You realise that?'

Medenhall's face was impassive, without obvious remorse or guilt. He spoke again.

'One other thing. Kinda odd. Tent was gone when I went back.'

Cal frowned.

'You're sure about that?'

'Unusual for it to be there in the first place. So I looked over that way. It was gone.'

'What sort of time you reckon that was?'

'One thirty, two am?'

'That's odd. Why would she leave at that time?'

'Figured she must've wanted to make an early start. Or someone gave her a lift or something.'

'So you knew it was a she?'

'Guess I did.'

'But you've not mentioned that before, either.'

'Like I said. The memory, not kicked in. She didn't pay her fee, either.'

Cal shook her head, bamboozled.

'A fiver. To cover rubbish and maintenance. Council won't come out this far. So we charge five dollars a night. Informal camping. She left before paying. Missed the bonfire next night too. Paddy's Day.'

'You said someone gave her a lift. Lift to where? At that time of night. To be clear, within the time you left the pub and came back. What, forty-five minutes, one hour? The tent was there and then gone.'

'That's what I'm sayin.'

Cal heard a squeak inside her head as she ground her molars. Her stomach rose and hit the concrete block in her chest. She spoke slowly.

'So, if you'd spoken to this young woman about paying a fee, did that conversation happen in the bar or down on the grass bank? My point being, was anyone else privvy to that conversation? To her presence?'

Medenhall's mouth formed a grim pout and his gaze went to the ceiling.

'Mmm. Got a feeling it might've been up here. Maybe out the back. Could've been taking empties out. Not sure sorry.'

'Really? You don't remember?'

Medenhall shrugged.

'Better get back,' he nodded along the bar.

'You know you're gonna skate for this?'

He averted his eyes, his pout grown more grave as he moved away.

Cal looked along the throng of drinkers on one side of the wooden sweep of the bar. On the other side, Troy Medenhall pulled a beer. His eyes momentarily her way, then back to the schooner he was filling.

Prick was lying. Not now? Why?

He's confirmed it though. I didn't imagine this scenario. He's confirmed Britta Kuiper was here.

Cal felt a fizz of excitement, despite the sombre nature of this latest revelation. She went over the details again. Early start to where? The ferry? Was Britta gonna walk to Wirriga Flat? Why not just wait til morning and hitch with a local? Most people passed through Wirriga heading for the city, she would be sure of a lift.

She immediately rang and updated Scobie. Medenhall would be getting a visit asap.

Back at her cabin, Cal lay on her bed without undressing. She stared into the darkness.

What happened in that hour or less in the middle of the night that made Britta leave?

Chapter 41

It was mid-afternoon as Cal worked on an area off the O'Rouke's Dam Track. This time she wasn't on the tops where she'd recently run into Tyra Huber, but further into the hinterland where the track dropped into an area of flatlands below the historic dam site.

Sediment control and erosion prevention were ongoing issues in the region where extreme flooding wasn't a new thing. But increased rainfall created new problems and, as a ranger, it was part of her remit to monitor anything relating to flood control. That included observation of the effects of feral animals eating the vegetation that held the ground together.

All morning she'd been thinking about Medenhall's revelations the previous night. She wanted desperately to speak more with Scobie but her ranger duties couldn't be continually shoved into the backseat. *Cal Nyx exercising patience and restraint. Break out the records ledger.*

She parked the truck in the lee of a sandstone cliff that offered some protection from the western sun. She loaded equipment into a small backpack and prepared to walk a large section of the flats, literally scanning the ground for animal scat and plant or soil damage. It might have seemed a mundane, pointless task of little value to most people. Trivial and base even. Cal felt anticipation, excitement and fascination.

After many hours of daylight the air was overheated and the atmosphere oppressive. The sun blared like a blast furnace. This was not the dry heat of the interior. In fact it felt like thunderstorm weather though the sky above the clearing was cloudless. She put on her wide-brimmed hat as she left the truck.

She traversed the area of low vegetation carrying an extendable pole to avoid having to constantly crouch down to identify pellets. Distinguishing scat was easy when you did it all the time. The size, shape and components of the droppings individuated the species. Smaller critters might leave behind indigestible insect pieces like wings. Wombat droppings were obvious - nothing else laid square pellets.

Cal had wandered a little over an hour and was on one knee beside an insect trap not far from the forest margin. She felt a sudden swaying as though the ground was a sprung floor wavering on its coil-springs. You need to drink more water mate, she chided herself.

Then the movement felt more like rolling, then an unpleasant jagging. Anxiety swamped her as she realised it was an earthquake. Something very familiar to those born in The Shaky Isles, her homeland. She looked up at her surrounds. No rock walls above. At that moment she heard a low-pitched rumble and thunderous whoomph several hundred metres away. *Really close.*

She looked towards where the sound came from as a cloud of yellow dust billowed from ground level and drifted towards the open plain. It emanated from right about where she'd parked the truck in the shade of a sandstone escarpment.

She remained close to the ground watching the dust drift across the clearing like a rolling, oche-coloured mist. Small rocks bounced and rattled off the cliff-sides as the fallen rock settled. Tremors continued beneath her, time lengthening between each series as she waited to see if the intensity would grow or diminish. Her stomach clenched like a claw around a solid rubber ball.

The bush was silent. A strange moment.

The air cleared as she waited, feeling puny, an insignificant cluster of conjoined atoms and particles in a universe she couldn't comprehend. She didn't dare approach the base of the cliff but her truck was under there somewhere. Even at distance she knew there was no way she would be able to dig it out. Possibly crushed, definitely undriveable, a write-off.

As the dust dispersed she gazed up at the rock wall that had dropped the outcrop. Diagonal striations were visible in the sedimentary rock face. Sandstone was porous and layered. It could absorb a lot of water which expanded when the cold was extreme. The changeable spring weather combined with the quake must have been enough to shake a weakened layer to part company with the rest of the rock face. She knew quakes happened in Australia, quite frequently even. It's just that most were negligible and rarely felt. How was her luck? Parking her truck in the lee of an outcrop that let go after how many thousands of years? The newly exposed rock seeing daylight for the first time in millennia. Her head swam at that idea. *Least I wasn't inside the cab.*

It was late afternoon. Too far to walk out and get to the O'Rourke's Dam Track and then further to the Lyrebird. Looked like she'd be spending a night in the bush. Best get a message to Fisho. Maybe someone could come and help next morning. They'd need a crew to free the truck. She held up her mobile. No signal. Her sat phone was in the truck cab. *Nice one.*

She looked at the sky above the western ridges. Heavy storm clouds had formed, blown from the coast. They capped the hinterland with an ominous pall. She was going to need some decent shelter. *Get to work, Nyx.* She had the water she carried, maybe 750 mls in her two containers. Better than nothing. But she'd need more, and food. Her primary concern however was shelter before nightfall.

She'd learnt a bit of Kiwi bush-craft when she'd taken off as a youngster. Honed and tweaked these same skills to suit Australian conditions. A bivvy in NZ, a gunyah in Aus. Same kinda thing, a rough, quick shelter. She wanted to stay well distant from the escarpment. Beyond the clearing, the area was edged with spotted gum forest, dappled with light. Further inland and close to the rock faces it became more damp, a tangled rainforest. She had maybe three and a half hours of daylight to gather materials, build a shelter, find water and food and make a fire. *No problemo.*

She walked along the margins of the forest searching for a spot that was flat without dangerous boughs above that could drop on her gunyah spot. Once she found a suitable area, she collected long, straight pieces of deadwood, about two metres in length. She cut standing deadwood of similar dimensions using the saw blade on her Leatherman tool. Though she only had her day pack with her and wasn't prepped for an overnight camp, the compact tool was always on her belt. Ditto the fire-stick on a lanyard around her neck. I kinda like this, she thought. An impromptu adventure. She accumulated sufficient timber then swept the ground clear of leaf litter using a couple of burrawang fronds. Explored the area for some suitable Y-branches from fallen boughs and added them to her stash.

At either end of the cleared area she dug out small holes using the end of a stick she'd sharpened to a point. It was slow, jarring work. She placed the first Y-branches at either end of the clearing as her uprights and then laid the longest horizontal branch across them. As she went to begin laying the sloping back supports the nascent construction collapsed.

She started again, this time firming up the Y-branches more and locking them together more carefully at opposing angles. Once all the back-poles were laid as an inclined wall, they were ready for a waterproofing cover of burrawang fronds. Thunder boomed in the distance. *Pick up the pace, Nyx.* Thirsty, tired and hungry, she quickly gathered material and laid it over the sloping wall.

***

After Cal's phone call regarding the conversation with Mitch Medenhall, Scobie set her alarm for 5am. The publican at The Bushman's Rest in Three Rivers had revealed information that cast several new slants on the investigation.

After a quick shower, Scobie dressed in her bedroom. On the plush carpet she stepped into her I'm-in-charge heels and glanced at the mirror, noting the perfect height of her court shoes. She slipped on the jacket of her dark grey suit and made one last check in the mirror, moving left, moving right. Gave herself a sly wink. *All in the shoulders, darling, all in the shoulders.*

Later at Richmond Command she stood and led the briefing.

'Okay everyone. Let's update.' She lifted her chin as the gathered officers became silent.

'First item. Mitch Medenhall, publican, has confirmed that Britta Kuiper was camped at Three Rivers the night before she supposedly left the area for Sydney.'

She paused.

'Obviously, if he's telling the truth, he's withheld information pertinent to a homicide. As it stands, he made this revelation to a third party. So it's currently hearsay. I want someone out there this morning to take a formal statement. Maybe you and Len.' Scobie nodded towards Janice Ottering and Birch. 'It's also possible he's scarpered, so be prepared for that. But the fact he's already admitted this sighting to someone on the periphery of this inquiry probably indicates he's going to front and take the consequences.'

Glen Avery looked at the floor. He resisted shaking his head and made no eye-contact with others in the room.

Claudia Rudnick glanced at Avery and bit down the urge to ask who the third-party was. She suspected it was Scobie's lover, Cal Nyx.

Another officer, Gavin Hassett, less nuanced - and less concerned with maintaining a silent disapproval of Scobie's love interest - spoke.

'Do we trust this Medenhall and the third-party? Who is it anyway? Why's Medenhall come clean now?'

Scobie's lips compressed. 'We're police, Gavin. Everyone lies to us. I think what's key here is, as you say, why has Medenhall come forth with this information now? What has prompted this admission? I can think of two possibilities right away.' She raised her eyebrows, challenging the officer to suggest his own or to continue probing at the identity of the third-party source.

When the briefing was over Scobie turned and left the room. Len Birch and Glen Avery both caught a glimpse of calf, bamboozled as Scobie's heels clicked across the flooring.

As she entered her office Scobie checked through her phone notifications. Where the hell was Cal?

***

Next item, water. A brackish lagoon had formed at one end of the main clearing, obviously fed by some source close to the escarpment. Cal found a creek bed beyond the main ponded area and followed it hoping to find better water.

She swept the area in front of her looking for red-bellied black snakes. Sure enough, as she was about to step over a log, she glimpsed a large red-belly basking at one end of the stump, its body stretched in the late afternoon sunlight. Cal, sluggish with dehydration and fatigue, knew all creatures needed water just as she did. She had to be alert.

She stepped back and sought a way around which necessitated approaching the creek from more dense vegetation where potential dangers wouldn't be so easy to spot. Despite her tiredness she back-tracked and searched for a more open approach to the water further away from her camp. She saw several more red-bellies before finding a flat, grassy patch of ground beside a tea-coloured pool. She filled her flask and sniffed at the water. She could smell the tannins but otherwise it seemed okay. Tempting as it was to just swill down the contents, she knew she had to wait until she'd purified it by boiling. The risk of infection would add to her woes if she didn't take that step.

Bedding material was next on the agenda. She set off again, combing the surrounds for wiwi, as they called it in NZ. A bushy green sedge that formed large clumps. She gathered thick armfuls cut from different plants so as not to deplete any individual one.

With her shelter complete she focussed on setting a small fire in front of the open side of her lean-to. The water she'd collected earlier needed boiling to purify it and she was desperate to hydrate. Every time she bent down she was dizzy as she rose and her feet were becoming clumsy. There was still time to collect bush tucker before the light faded. But getting dry tinder for the fire was critical.

She gathered fluffy material. With her tinder material puffed-up in a tiny pile on a tree stump, she ran the back of her knife blade down the bottom half of the striker. A small shower of sparks raced into the dry material. She gathered the soft handful into her bird's nest of string-bark and grass rubbings and held it aloft, blowing gently until she had a mini-fire in her hands which she placed into her prepared fire pit. She knelt and fed more kindling and sticks into the fire. Once she had a good blaze going she created a space for her stainless-steel water bottle and gazed into the flames as she waited for it to boil. There was something so primal and comforting about fire, a contained one at least. It provided warmth and light, deterred predators, cooked food and purified water. What wasn't there to love, she thought. Still, in that environment, it could also wreck the most unimaginable damage.

She added more sticks. When the water boiled, she used two sticks like tongs to remove it from the fire. Now she had to wait for it to cool. Probably best to gather some bush food if she could find any. The two protein bars in her day pack weren't going to sustain her for long. But it was beyond her, shoulders aching from the digging and sawing she'd done earlier. *You're so outa condition, Nyx.* At least if she could sleep she'd be fresher in the morning. And sleep was all she wanted. Sitting back on her haunches she poked at the fire, her eyelids heavy with exhaustion. She drank half the water from her cooled steel bottle and watched through the trees as the sky turned into colours that repeated those in the centre of the fire in front of her. The sun dropped below the dark silhouette of the distant escarpment. She tipped her water bottle upright and drained the last of it.

Leaving some of her stashed wood for morning she stoked the fire and rolled into her shelter.

Chapter 42

CHARLIE STONE WONDERED ABOUT her own farm and that of her neighbour. How on earth did a freezer end up buried on her property? And when she'd opened it and found what looked shockingly like human remains, well, she didn't put it there. Did her mum or dad do that? Nonsense. Who did that leave? The brother. Didn't need to ponder that one for long. But did wonder over the following days as she fought the panic of having that thing there, so close. Thought long on where else it might have come from. Thought about the conditions under which she'd found it. The flood. Remembered previous high water events. One in particular when a neighbour had cleared the channel with a back-hoe when the waters threatened the house. Clearing the channel and tidying the mess of debris from the banks. Neighbourly.

Who associated with that place could do this? Old man Pinder was a gnarly prick. Wouldn't put anything past him. What state was he in back then? Might've been a bit frail.

What about Hugh? Bit of a non-descript. He was away a lot studying. Then he was fully away overseas. What do they say about the quiet ones? Couldn't really see it though.

Did they have help on the farm?

Yeh Charlie, they did. Your own brother.

Mm. Dear Gordon. Now there's a candidate. Spineless and shifty.

Your own flesh and blood, Charlie.

Yup. Been in WA a long, long time. Good spot for a psycho, the mines. Good ol Gordy.

Okay, she wouldn't put it past him. But why would he put a body in a freezer and bury it on his own family property when there were thousands of miles of bush nearby? Seemed too risky. Maybe not her dodgy brother then. So, who? Old man Pinder was dead twenty-odd years. Nope. Her own father dead before that. Who was left?

Hugh Pinder.

She shuffled a series of images through her mind. Some went way, way back, to childhood. The gangling youth. Their farm or her own home, a free-for-all movement between the properties across the bridge.

His "game", locking her in the freezer in their shed. Not her idea of fun. Claustrophobic ever since. She'd pulled a clasp from her hair and scratched her initials in the plastic floor in case he never let her out. Hugh was all smiles when he eventually did release her. "Just a game". Obviously she'd convinced herself of that too. Once the terror dissipated. Had never really considered it again.

A freezer.

Hugh Pinder.

Now it was front and centre. And more recollections popped up in the wake of the others. Wasn't it around the same time she'd taken a bucket of raspberries over for their neighbours? Mrs Pinder away, old man Pinder already passed. Hugh there on a uni break but unsighted. Charlie went to put the fruit in the Pinder's outside freezer so it wouldn't spoil before they returned. But the freezer was gone. When she rang later to tell Hugh he'd said the motor had broken down. He'd taken it to the tip.

***

On the South Coast Dif's shoulders slumped with a heavy lassitude as he listened to Tambor's rambling. A small fire of irritation stirred inside Dif but his body was bowed in a sluggish resignation borne through years of taking the crap.

He could smell the brine of the ocean also carrying the scent of granite dust from the quarry.

'Why'd you bring me here? To scare me? You bore me, copper. Get it over with,' Dif drawled.

Tambor flicked his ciggy butt. It arced then blew back in the air current pushed up from the swells hitting the rock face below.

'A simple request. I asked you to drop the complaint against me.' Tambor folded his arms, the cumbersome plastered arm topmost.

Dif puffed out a frustrated sigh. 'You should think about a new career. Though I imagine you'll indulge your uninformed theories wherever you land.'

He looked directly into Tambor's eyes. 'I'm not dropping the complaint. People like me have always been here. We're not going away.'

'Let's take a little walk.' Tambor stepped backwards, indicating Dif should go first.

'I'm not one for random exercise,' Dif countered.

'C'mon. Wanna show you something.' Tambor moved closer.

In the darkness the rhythmic rumble of the swell pounded into the base of the cliffs. Dif felt the low-pitched vibration through the veneer of vegetation underfoot.

'I'm good right here,' he said.

Tambor grabbed Dif's arm and dug his fingers deep into the wiry triceps muscle, shoving Dif forward. He followed up with an instep aimed at the back of Dif's knee. The resulting stumble a reminder of who was in charge.

Dif in a cold, lonely cell in a quiet coastal police station just kilometres away. Impossible to feel anything but powerlessness inside the cage. Tambor the sole jailer that night. His toxic fascination introduced to Dif several years before.

Now Dif scuffed along the track edging the fallaway, Tambor prodding him ahead with judicious shoves. This wasn't going to end well.

The briny air was cool on his skin and sharp in his nostrils. It awoke something in Dif and heightened some profound instinct. He loved this coast. The quiet and solitude of the nearby bush, the whales and dolphins that plied the waters offshore. He'd loved the humble bush retreat he built before he'd had to leave in fear for his very existence. A killer had precipitated that departure. But Tambor's malign attentions had been part of the mix then too. A languor, calcified and marrow-deep at each successive conflict involving Tambor, began to crumble as an equally historic fury frothed from somewhere subterranean. It rose through his body, minute fissures combusting as it gained oxygen and lifted his energy with an explosive burst.

Dif bent his knees and dropped low as he twisted on the balls of his feet and spun backwards. He threw his head and shoulders into Tambor's mid-section and drove upwards with his thighs, lifting Tambor off and over the cliff side.

Dif stumbled as the weight released, his palms and one knee ground against the gritty rock of the track. Rasping breath stung his throat as the stark moment pinned him to the ground.

Get outa here.

Tambor's cries dissipated with the sea-mist, lost in the roar and tumble of rollers smashing against sandstone.

Dif didn't tarry. He turned and scrabbled up the track towards the carpark.

Funny, being there. His old stomping ground. The quarry along by the river and the remains of his old camp down there in the darkness somewhere. The rail lines crossing the water.

He walked the familiar route and headed for Greyridge station.

A train to Sydney would come by in the morning.

***

Now that Jessica Barson had a flowered tent-fly embedded in her mind, another noteworthy feature of that day surfaced. Her grandpop's last birthday. He'd come that afternoon for cake and she'd become the focus of attention because of her poor, battered knee.

So, it must have been 17th March, 1996.

She rang Charlie Stone and asked for Cal's number.

Then she rang Cal. It went to voice mail.

'Cal, I've remembered something. It's really freaked me out. Please call.'

Chapter 43

CAL CLOSED HER EYES. Now she was horizontal and still her stomach cramped and grumbled with hunger. She fantasized over the cans of beans and packets of dehy in her survival kit. In the truck. Should have spent more time foraging. She'd be walking out tomorrow. Why worry? Roots and seeds and berries. She knew enough to keep from starving. But it was near impossible to go for long without protein. She had the hidden rifle in a closed tube under the truck. Only had to scrape away two tons of rubble using her hands to get at it. *Is this delirium?*

Could she shoot and kill something? Or trap a critter? Yabbies in a creek. Good water required for that scenario. Eels if she was in NZ. Make a trap or a bone hook, unseen in a hunk of rancid roadkill or whatever you might term the incidental death of something out here. Not that a carcass lasted for long. Find a piece of bone from a small animal skeleton, smash it with a rock until you had a small section. File the ends down to sharp points. Make a thin twine from long fibres rolled and twisted. Dianella perhaps. Have to make a shell scraper first or something similar to clean off the fleshy green stuff. Tie the twine around an indent you've cut into the centre circumference of the bone. That would take some doing, cutting that. Attach the thin twine to a thicker plaited twine you've made, a longer one you attach to the bank, a tree trunk or root. Chuck it in the water and come back next day for eel steaks. *Easy peasy. Yeh, sure. And Cal, you've never eaten eel.*

She gazed out through the open side to the sky beyond the treetops, clear and star-studded. Her shoulders ached. Her eyes were scratchy and heavy with tiredness as she closed them and listened to the bush sounds. Her tinnitus bad. Ringing and high-pitched, a sign of stress. How could she be stressed in the bush? She focused on the noises outside of her head.

Lot of bird action. Breeding season. Territorial and looking for mates. The repeated whoo-whoo-whoo of a tawny frogmouth, and much further in the distance, the double hoot of the hawk-owl, Ninox strenua, the Powerful Owl. Ground level sounds too. Scratching and sweeping. Little critters. She calmed her intake of the cool air and relaxed her fingers.

Ran her mind across several pieces of information. The sudden emergency had given her a reprieve from the case but now she pondered something sticky about that last night when Britta Kuiper was at Three Rivers. And the only people who spoke of seeing her in that twelve-hour period were the publican and the doctor.

Neither of their stories could be corroborated. Medenhall said the tent was missing at about 2am. Why would he say that if it wasn't true? Because it meant if something happened to Britta, it happened while he was with his mystery woman. And whoever she was, she couldn't confirm the story because she met him under the bridge. No view to the part of the riverbank by the picnic table.

Medenhall could've done the deed on Britta Kuiper and removed all trace of her after he met with his woman and no one, apparently, had seen him. And why had he come forward with this story now? Because Cal was asking questions? The police were asking questions? He needed to cover his ass. But it had only come to light recently when the body was found. Prior to that, no one knew that Britta Kuiper had never arrived in Sydney. No one knew that she had disappeared. He had nothing to hide beyond his affair.

But what if he was telling the truth?

It would mean that Britta Kuiper was gone that night. Either she'd left of her own accord, which defied logic, or someone had disposed of Britta and her belongings while Medenhall was downriver. And if that were the case then Hugh Pinder couldn't have given Britta a lift next morning, which is what he had always maintained. He didn't give her a lift because he'd done away with her. He was lying.

Hang on. Go back. It wasn't logical for Britta to leave in the middle of the night, to de-camp and take off. Unless she was scared off. Why would she set-up camp then re-pack and leave after midnight? It was only something you'd do if you absolutely had to. And where would she go then? Where would feel safe? Where could she overnight? It was certainly another possibility. Britta could've just holed up in the bush until daylight and then carried on with her plan to head to Sydney. After all, she was a young woman who'd traveled to the opposite end of the globe on her own. She wasn't without ability. That scenario had to be kept on the table.

Otherwise, one or both were lying.

Or Medenhall and Pinder might be working together. Her mind wound tight and twisted until it hurt. A maze she couldn't unravel in her overtaxed state. It was all conjecture. She still had nothing concrete that bound all the pieces together. She heard scratching nearby. Short bursts of rapid digging then pausing. Something small. Bandicoot maybe. *Cool.*

And lulled by that scraping refrain she drifted off.

Minutes later the crack of overhead lightning had her cowering in her gunyah. The boom of thunder reverberated off the cliff faces as she drew her arms around her ears. Beyond her shelter the surrounds bleached in a split-second of harsh white illumination like a shadowbox image.

Heavy raindrops spattered on the fronds above her. Then the downpour came. Didn't take long to prove her shelter wasn't quite waterproof. She squished herself into the driest corner and tucked her stash of tinder material inside her shirt. Kicked her firewood back under her heels.

At some point, the storm passed. She wavered in and out of exhaustion and partial sleep. That half-delirium, falling forward sensation.

The Yowie thing Lola had seen. The rubber mask. Why was there a rubber mask with the body? It made no sense. Unless it was somehow related to the murder. Had the killer worn the mask as a way of hiding their identity? But no one she'd spoken to had ever mentioned such a thing. It was so random.

She gave up on sleep. It was still dark. She lit a new fire, gazed into the flames. A campfire. The campers. Magic mushrooms and distorted reality. Wavering flames and seaweed moving underwater. A hirsute monster. The Yowie. Was the Yowie someone wearing a gorilla mask? Was that it? So creepy.

Could someone who was part of the camping group have snuck away from the camp or would they have been noticed? Was it someone who knew of the camping group but wasn't part of it? Someone older? Bigger? An adult who knew where they were going to camp. Someone who got off on scaring a young woman, a teenager. Really, really creepy. Someone who perhaps graduated to killing a different young woman several years later.

Cal shook herself. That moment when she looked inside the freezer, the sight of that thing. The mask. And the smell. It all haunted her. But more than that, the idea someone tried to scare that young girl, Lola. And that mask was with the body of another young woman. A dead one.

She needed to get back to Three Rivers. Real quick. Without a truck. *Couple of k's up the incline, maybe five more k's to the end of O'Rourke's at the Lyrebird Track. N'other ten k's to Three Rivers. Maybe seven more to Charlie's. 'Bout twenty-five k's all up. Won't be walkin all of that. No time. Five k per hour, couple hours I can walk to the Lyrebird at least.*

She packed up, covered her fire and started walking as the sun rose and the bird calls competed for airtime.

Chapter 44

CAL TRUDGED WITH PURPOSE past her truck. The rear corner of the deck the only part visible under the rock and debris that had settled in a ochre-coloured mound. She made her way back up the track she'd driven in on the day before and held her phone up to check her signal. Thirty percent battery left. No bars. *Try again at the top.* She walked on the shady side. Needed a vehicle asap. Needed Scobie and the crew. Needed Dif, anyone. No, not anyone. *Vehicle. Headache. Caffeine.*

Close to the top of the incline a series of notifications pinged on her phone. *Finally, some signal.*

One of the texts was from Pirate. She'd set Pirate an urgent task when she'd visited. She opened that text first.

-Previous property owner you requested: Laurence Raymond Pinder.

Fuuuuckk.

Cal's brain pinged and swirled.

She'd asked Pirate to check a land register for the property across the bridge from Charlie Stone's place. Laurence Pinder must be Hugh Pinder's father.

Far out. So Hugh would've grown up there.

Cal's empty stomach heaved. Her skin was sticky with grit and sweat, her head woolly and aching from dehydration.

Cal and Scobie had ascertained the property was sold in 2009 when they saw the sales info the other day. If Britta Kuiper had gone missing twenty five years ago and been buried on Charlie's property, then the Pinder ownership at that time was potentially damning.

The diggings on the stream bed at Charlie Stone's and the recent flooding. Charlie's odd behaviour at that last book club. Charlie must've found the damn freezer. Charlie must've moved it. Why?

Cal picked up her pace along O'Rourke's Dam Track. Her exhaustion, thirst and hunger pushed aside as disturbing ideas crystallised.

Charlie figured out it was Pinder because he used to be her neighbour. Couldn't have been anyone else and Charlie knew it. Charlie moved the thing because she was scared. Too scared to go to the cops. Charlie took that perilous option rather than risk Hugh Pinder's wrath. Because she was familiar with it?

Yeh. The evidence was there in front of her when she opened that freezer.

Cal checked her phone signal again. One to two bars. Texts might get through. Calls unlikely.

Charlie's in danger. Message Scobie. Message Charlie.

-Charlie. Get out. Leave your place NOW. Trust me. Cal.

One to Scobie.

-Send patrol to Charlie Stone's. Urgent.

No wonder Charlie was weird that night at the meet up. Slightly drunk or unhinged or something. Woman must've been crapping herself.

Cal needed to get to Charlie.

Charlie knew who the killer was. She wasn't protecting him. That was incidental. She was protecting herself. Getting that white tomb off her property.

Cal held her phone up again. She'd walked maybe two k's, the road still sloping uphill towards the eventual junction with The Lyrebird Track. Several more kilometres away. Dying for water.

The track flattened slightly on a ridge. Cal pictured the road in at the junction of the Lyrebird Track. One farm on the northern side. Maybe she could borrow a vehicle? Worth a try. Had to do something. She thumbed another few texts as she strode along O'Rourke's Dam Track.

Her boss, Fisho.

-Truck written off in rockfall. More later.

One to Dif as well. What the hell. It was all hands on deck even if Dif was in Sydney.

Cops would be an hour away minimum if they'd left from Richmond asap.

She trudged on. Tried to run, breath ripping at her dry throat.

Half an hour later on her right, a driveway to the only farm she knew of in that area. The farmhouse visible two hundred metres beyond on a hillock.

Water and vehicle her internal mantra as her leaden legs lifted and planted. She was fit from her work, but lack of sleep, water and food were compromising her already diminished reserves.

The homestead was brick, long and low with a deep veranda facing west. Cal knocked at the front door. Stepped back, waited. No response. She raced around to the rear of the house and called out.

Saw a tap and hose attached to the back wall. Knelt down and fed water down her throat, over her head. Unclipped the carabiner and filled her empty bottle then stood and called again. Nothing.

A low open-fronted four-bay shed stood across one side of the yard adjacent to the house. Cal scanned the contents.

Tractor. *Nah, too slow.* Quad bike. *Maybe. Low-gearing, not real fast. Better than nothing.* She sprinted over. *Key in the ignition, great.* She twisted the fuel cap off and shook the machine. Low on gas. Looked around the shed. Found several fuel containers against the side wall. One marked four-stroke only. Topped up the tank on the quad. Looked around for a helmet. Nothing. Wasn't keen on riding the roads without one but, *fuck it.*

She fired the machine up and stomped it into first. Rode around to the front door. Charged over and pulled an old receipt and pencil from her tote. "Emergency. Borrowed your quad. Will sort later. Thanks."

Secured the note under a pot plant and took off.

Chapter 45

CAL SKITTERED THE QUAD bike out of the farm driveway. Her relief at finding a vehicle competing with alarm over fears for Charlie Stone. She hit the tarmac of The Lyrebird Track and headed for Three Rivers. The machine was low-geared which meant the engine was screaming flat-out in top-gear but at least it beat walking.

Wind rushed past her ears and the air around her body felt exhilarating but frightening in the absence of any head or body protection.

She glanced at the speedo. Eighty kph with the throttle wide open. *Whatevs.*

She swept through the Three Rivers village and hit the brakes as she approached the bridge. Putting the quad sideways she righted the steering and sped across.

It was less than five ks to Charlie's farm. Cal didn't have a weapon. She didn't have help.

She'd messaged Dif but he was two hours away in Sydney as far as she knew. Scobie and the crew were still at least a half hour away if they'd left straight away when she'd messaged.

You're gonna have to wing it, Nyx.

She visualised the layout at Charlie's. The drive to the house. No surprise or subterfuge via that way in. What about the stream that passed the front of the house?

Ready for a dip?

But she didn't know the stream. Why not park beyond Charlie's place and walk in? That could be stealthy, she told herself.

She switched off the machine and coasted along the road edge well before Charlie's driveway entrance. Further along the roadway, parked in the shadows of an acacia thicket, Cal spotted the rear of an SUV.

A dark blue SUV.

He's already here. I hope I'm not too late.

Her guts roiled, churning an acidic emptiness. She swallowed as she leapt off the quad, looking all around as if Pinder might be waiting to ambush her.

He's parked outside, not driven up to her house. That's dodgy right?

She scuttled along to the SUV. Looked in through the rear window. No one inside. Went to the front and touched the hood. Warm, and the vehicle was in the shade. Maybe she was still in time.

She darted back towards the driveway. Insects chirruped in the undergrowth. There was no nearby traffic noise. If Pinder was already there, he could've heard her arrival. Assuming he wasn't already inside with Charlie.

Move it. And you're still unarmed and approaching someone who's killed before.

Through gaps in the shrubbery she could see light glancing off the surface of the windows at the front corner of the house. She snuck along the edge of the graveled drive, aware of the sound of her own footfalls. Unavoidable. She could smell the gums that towered behind the house, the leaf resins super-heated during the morning and releasing their scent. An overlay of jasmine that draped a trellis on the edge of the rear side garden, almost headache-inducing with its sweetness.

As Cal got closer to the house she crouched and paused in the shadowed margins of the driveway shrubbery. Now she could hear music playing, perhaps something Charlie put on while she made lunch. Classical, not something Cal could recognise since it was beyond the realms of blues, reggae and funk. Where was Pinder?

No voices from inside.

Cal tuned her ear back outside the house then heard the distinct low snap of a small branch underfoot. Something or someone in the shrub border that edged the house. Not on the soft lawn, not on the driveway or paths. She strained her hearing to pinpoint the source of the sound. Around by the French doors?

She still needed a weapon. She had nothing. No Ninja training, nothing. A rock or a lump of wood was better than nothing. She had her trusty Leatherman. She placed her hand on the belt-sheath for reassurance. Wasn't keen on using a small knife but would if she had to. Fumbled the dome clasp of the pouch open.

Chapter 46

THE MUSIC FROM INDOORS was louder. One of the French doors was ajar.

Cal scanned the grounds beyond then back to the borders adjoining the house. Still no voices. What had she heard outside before then. An animal? Why was the door ajar? *Have a look, Nyx.*

Cal crept closer to the house. Drew her Leatherman tool and unlocked the handles. Her thumbnail swung out the longest knife blade. All whilst keeping her eyes on the interior of the house.

She reached the glass door and peered inside. Her knife hand down beside her thigh.

Across the room in the kitchen she saw Hugh Pinder behind the bench. No sign of Charlie.

Pinder looked up. Cal was directly in his sight line, illuminated by the daylight behind her.

'Where is she?' Cal demanded.

Pinder stood motionless for a beat then moved out from the bench towards Cal.

'Oh, hi. You looking for Charlie too?' Pinder's tone was light and friendly, ignoring Cal's strident request.

Cal watched his hands as she took another step into the room.

Pinder's long legs took him across the space in three strides, a neutral smile on his lips.

'She must be in the garden,' he said lunging at Cal. Both his hands aimed at her throat.

The force of his moving mass knocked her backwards. Her heel caught on the doorstep. Her left arm flailed at his right forearm. His left hand grabbed her neck.

Cal's right hand was free. As she fell backwards she gripped tight on the Leatherman handle and drove the blade in an arc. Up and in, targetting his kidneys. It was a short blade but like all her tools it was very sharp.

Her head hit the flagstones, a thudding crack as she blanked out.

Chapter 47

THE POLICE FOUND PINDER partway along the drive at Charlie Stone's property where he'd collapsed trying to get to his vehicle. One officer rang for an ambulance while another applied emergency first aid to Pinder's knife wound.

Paramedics arrived nearly forty minutes later. Pinder was stretchered away to the nearest ED in Windsor.

Cal regained a groggy consciousness soon after police arrived. She was allowed to remain at the scene having been assessed by a paramedic and told to rest.

Scobie, in charge of the operation, had asked Constable Ruddick to phone Cal's landlord, Dee, who came within the hour and took Cal home.

Officers searched the property for Charlie Stone without result. She and her vehicle were missing. Scobie had Richmond Command release an APB including a public announcement for sightings of Charlie Stone. She also assigned an officer to secure Pinder's hospital room post surgery, awaiting his release for questioning.

***

Next day, Scobie was in her office briefing the prosecutor when she took an urgent call.

Charlie Stone had walked into a police station in Port Macquarie and sought assurance that Hugh Pinder was in custody. She'd asked to speak with the OIC of the body in the freezer case. Charlie confessed to Scobie that it was she who'd dumped the freezer off The Lyrebird Track. She'd put the padlock on hoping the contents would never be seen again. She said that she was prepared to come in and face the consequences and Scobie promised her that her safety was paramount. The police wanted to cooperate with her and get a positive outcome for Britta Kuiper and her family.

Scobie then had a private conversation with the prosecutor who wondered if, despite Charlie moving the freezer, mitigation could be a factor. Charlie had interfered with evidence of a crime. But the sheer terror resulting from uncovering Pinder's deeds drove her to it. She'd quickly figured out that only Pinder could have done this. And she knew that he would know she was the only one who could have worked that out. She'd always been aware that he was shady but she'd had no idea he could actually kill." Alright for those cops safe in town, slowly building their case against him. I'm the one who's got to live out here with the bastard on my flippin doorstep. Hmm. Nice country doctor. Not like he won't get bail pending investigations. And who am I? The prey, waiting. Nah." The only way Charlie saw to protect herself in the immediate moment was to hide his crime so he wouldn't come for her next. Her hand was forced by circumstance. Of course it would be up to her counsel to establish whether this was the case. She may not get off scot-free but, privately, it was felt police were unlikely to pursue a harsh penalty for Charlie who had inadvertently brought the original crime to light.

When Scobie got a chance she phoned Cal to let her know that Charlie was safe.

'She got your message to get out, Cal. She just grabbed her keys and her cards and left the house. She didn't risk leaving via Three Rivers. She took back routes to the other side of the Hawkesbury and headed North. She wanted me to thank you.'

The following day at Richmond Command Cal waited in the carpark for Scobie. She'd borrowed Dee's old Datsun sedan and sat thumbing through Rat Rodders Weekly. She wore dark sunnies and had taken medication for the after-effects of her head knock.

When Scobie walked from the building with a water bottle in one hand, Cal got out and hugged the DI. Scobie leaned against the car, turned her face to the sky, shaded her eyes.

'Well, he's come clean. He's given everything up. That doesn't happen often. Apparently he's been on all sorts of prescription meds for quite a while. I think he's quite addled from that. Plus years of living with the secret. The burden of it. He says it was an accident. Either way, if he'd been caught back then, accident or not, he would've done significant jail time.'

'Did he explain how exactly it was an accident?' Cal put emphasis on the last word, her tone ironic.

Scobie sipped from her water bottle. 'Pinder says he'd seen Britta Kuiper early that evening in The Bushman's Rest. Saw her speaking to Mitch Medenhall, the publican. When she'd left and gone outside he followed moments later. Saw her go through the carpark and down the bank to the picnic area. He watched her begin setting up her tent at dusk. He went back inside the pub and had a few drinks. Went home, stewed, my term, came back after closing time. His home at that time was five ks away. Across the stream from Charlie's as we now know. He says he went to the tent and asked her if she wanted to share a joint. Chatted with her. He put the hard word on her and she told him she wasn't into blokes. He persisted, they struggled ...'

'Fuck's sake. She made the mistake of being friendly and she ends up dead. How can that be an accident?'

'Yep. Attempted rape may well be added to the list of charges. We may never know for sure what went down. But Britta is dead. It's just a horrible, tragic mess.'

'What was the significance of the mask? Did that come up?'

'It did. He says he'd worn it a couple of years prior to the incident with Britta, trying to scare some kids in the bush.'

'Ugh. What a freak.'

Scobie shrugged. 'When he went to move the freezer, the mask was behind it, where he'd tossed it all those years before. He just threw it inside the freezer and carried on with moving and burying it.'

Cal shook her head. 'So, it was a total furphy?'

'Well, trying to scare those younger kids, indicates something doesn't it?'

Cal remembered Lola's story and her fright retelling it, even after all that time. 'Creepy,' she muttered. She gazed unfocused into the distance, a queasiness in her stomach. She wanted to move, to escape. 'You free to leave now, Scobes?'

'I can take a bit of a break. Let's go to yours, huh. Oh, and I meant to tell you something earlier. So much going on I forgot.' Scobie explained about the initials scratched inside the freezer, something clarified after speaking with Charlie Stone. 'So they preceded Britta's body being in there,' Scobie finished.

Cal drew in a deep breath. 'That's a relief. Sort of. Like, Britta not being buried alive. Still frickin' horrible. All of it. Must've been bloody awful for young Charlie. What an asshole that bloke is.'

They continued their conversation later at Cal's place in Kurrajong.

'You think he's gonna try for Involuntary Manslaughter?' Cal said as she held the fridge door open and gathered some nibbles and drinks.

'I have no idea what his lawyer will suggest but that's a strong possibility. He also attacked you, Cal. Prosecution will be adding Attempted Murder for that, or Grievous Bodily Harm at a minimum.'

'Not keen on court, Scobes. Keep me out of it.' She tipped olives into a small dish. 'So, you don't reckon he did this to anyone else?'

Scobie shrugged.

'He took a life. He's a weirdo and somewhat unpleasant, but I don't think he's a serial murderer. They don't give themselves up. Their egos don't allow for that. There may have been just the one incident.'

'Incident? You mean murder.'

'Well, that's to be established. It's a homicide, obviously. Prosecution will need to show intent.'

'You reckon one and done?' Cal placed a tall glass of water in front of Scobie, lemon wedges and mint leaves floating amongst ice-cubes.

'I know, it's a horrible expression. Such an offhand way to describe the taking of a life.'

'Guess they need an alternative to spree murders or whatever. It does kinda point to the possibility of an accident I guess.'

'The murderer wasn't driven to repeat the act.' Scobie did quote marks in the air. 'As in, there was no pleasure in it, he didn't pursue that payoff? Not that we know of anyway. Still, under our laws, he committed the most grave of crimes. And his profession as well. Not a good look.'

'Yeh, and it's not exactly harmless putting your hands around someone's neck and squeezing until they go limp.'

'Trending contemporary sexual game-play notwithstanding.'

'Well, that's another interesting backlash, isn't it?' Cal said.

'How do you mean?' Scobie sipped her water.

'This murder happened decades ago. Feminism had gained a little toehold. Again. And by the next decade, it's a fun, edgy, sex-game to strangle your partner.'

'Well, the law has recognised that putting hands around someone's neck is a precursor to domestic violence deaths.'

'Eventually. And we're not talking about reciprocal sex-play here. It's women getting strangled. Look, I'm not averse to a bit of rough stuff ...'

'Swoon.'

'Stop it.'

Cal looked away, turned back towards Scobie, eyes not meeting hers.

'Bloke did it to me once. Not a sex thing. Obviously. It was a work situation, when I was fourteen. My foreman, this big guy, six three. He just clamps his hands around my neck and squeezes and fucking lifts me off the ground,' Cal paused, 'and I can't do anything. I can't yell, I can't breathe, I can't speak. And he's like shaking me, gripped on and laughing.'

Scobie stared.

'I thought I was gonna die. The most terrifying part was I couldn't make a sound. No traction with the ground. My hands grabbing at his arms and he thinks it's funny. And I can't fucking tell him, it's not. Or maybe he didn't think it was funny. Maybe his laughing was that anxious, guilty, I'm-enjoying-this-too-much-and-I can't-stop kind of reaction.'

Cal's right hand had gone to her own throat as though protecting it.

'Jesus Cal.' Scobie touched Cal's arm.

'I reckon they know they're immune. If you're in a household with no adult male they figure you're easy pickings. And you are really. No father. No drama. The predators' home in on that.'

Scobie drew her into a hug. Cal, stiff in her embrace. A mix of anger and sadness seeping through her body.

Cal drew back.

'I was dealing with that shit since I was about nine or ten. It was my world. My normal. I thought everyone grew up with that. Anyway,' she mumbled, 'I need some air. Going outside for a bit.'

Cal crossed the gravelled yard to the darkness of an open, lean-to shed. She wanted to smash something. To hear the shattering noise of metal on glass, steel hammering on tin, anything, heavy, sharp, brutal.

But she didn't want Scobie to get wind of that across the yard in the sleepout.

She leaned against a workbench. Her shoulders and arms zinged with a charge, like the sky before a thunderstorm. A dark energy that needed dissipating. There was something else under all the firy angst anyway. Something altogether different. Deeper, older.

A grey exhaustion drew her down to the floor. She crouched beneath the workbench, her arms tight around her knees as she ground her eyes into the fabric of her jeans. Sobbing over a tiny wail as she rocked on her heels.

Inside the sleepout, Scobie rang the Richmond team for overnight updates on the investigation. Avery had news that Britta Kuiper's parents had been contacted in The Netherlands. They had confirmed a fracture to Britta's left leg when she was younger. The Kuipers agreed to having DNA swabs taken by local Politie and sent to Richmond Command for confirmation of her identity. They were unsure whether they wanted Britta's remains returned to them, a notion that Scobie found disturbing when she was told.

'Anything yet from the search at the old Pinder farm?' she asked Avery.

'Yeh actually. Team there going through the oldest shed. Although the folks who bought the place said it was mostly cleared of larger items, machinery and what-not, there were a few cobwebby boxes under a workbench. One was full of rusty nails and bolts, the other had ancient electrical stuff in it. Old heating elements and Bakelite switch housings. Wire and stuff. Seems old man Pinder threw nothing away.'

'Cut to the chase, Glen.'

'An electrical plug. Snipped off with its wires intact.'

'The freezer plug, you think?'

'It's been bagged and sent for testing. If the cuts in the wire match the piggy-back plug on the freezer – which wasn't original – it's pretty damning.'

'Places the freezer at the Pinder property. Great work, Glen. Fingers crossed on that. And please pass on my thanks to the officers who did the search. Keep in touch, I'll be in soon.'

Sometime later, minutes, an hour, she couldn't tell which, Cal returned inside the cabin. Scobie was standing at the kitchenette.

'You okay, hon?' Scobie asked.

Cal went to her, they hugged.

They were both silent for several moments.

'Wonder what Fisho's gonna say when they find my rifle?'

'You've lost me.'

'Under my truck. When they haul it out from the rockfall and assess the damage. Sure it'll be a write-off. My rifle's stashed in a tube under the deck.'

'Of course. Not work-issue equipment, right?'

'Right.'

'Nothing you can do for now though.'

'Could go up there with a Bobcat and dig it out myself. Retrieve the Remington before they find it.'

'I need to get back to the investigation, hon. I've only got an hour max. By the way. I had a thought. He's not one-and-done. Pinder, I mean.'

'Huh.'

'Pinder. He was going to kill Charlie Stone. Maybe he didn't kill anyone else in the interim. He may not have been propelled by a murderous impulse for those intervening years. But he was ready to deal with Charlie. Permanently. He was prepared to kill again to cover up the first death. He'd crossed that line before. He was prepared to do it again.'

'Yeh. I see what you mean.'

'And he attacked you as well. Sadly, it's not an uncommon scenario. A second or even third murder to cover up some previous nefarious deed.'

'Does my head in,' Cal said. She rubbed a hand across the back of her neck.

'Mm hmm.'

Cal slapped her thighs.

'Let's do something fun.'

'What do you have in mind?'

'A reckless drive to nowhere. Brunch en-route.'

'Done.' Scobie's eyebrows lifted. 'Have you had concussion before?'

'A few.'

'How 'bout I drive?'

Acknowledgements

Thank you to the readers who have left their thoughts and responses to my stories in reviews. You are the reason I do this.

Thank you, Biz Hayman, for the evocative cover design, editorial feedback and DI Liz Scobie secret-lady-business insights.

Thank you Tracey Savage for close-reading, editorial input and general expertise. Your feedback is always invaluable and spot-on.

Thank you Marian Evans for unswerving support and for being a member our our little collective.

Thanks to some fav YouTube channels for fun and inspiration, Vice Grip Garage and Scotty's Gone Walkabout.

About the author

Kim Hunt's debut crime novel, *TheBeautiful Dead*, introduced her kick-ass, can-do protagonist, park ranger Cal Nyx. It was released in 2020 by Bloodhound Books UK and was shortlisted for Best First Novel in the 2021 Ngaio Marsh Awards. Her second-in-series Cal Nyx mystery, *The Quarry*, was published under the Spiral Collectives imprint in mid-2023. It was longlisted for the 2023 Ngaio Marsh Awards for Best Crime Novel.

Kim was named runner-up in the US-based Sisters in Crime 2023 Pride Awards for Emerging LGBTQIA+ Crime Writers.

A standalone novel set in NZ, *The Corrector*, will be published in early 2025.

Proudly working-class, Kim spent the 1990s as a floor and wall tiler in Sydney while studying as a mature-age undergrad student. She's also worked as a band roadie, a women's refuge worker and a gardener in both Australia and Aotearoa (New Zealand), where she was born. She's lived in gritty urban environments and outside under corro in the Australian bush. She's also done a lot of cross-country road miles despite a period of being nailed down to complete a Master of Letters at the University of Sydney.

Kim currently lives and writes in Aotearoa, NZ.

The Beautiful Dead, first in the Cal Nyx series, published in 2020, shortlisted for Best First Novel in the 2021 Ngaio Marsh Awards.

The Quarry, second in Cal Nyx series, published in 2023, longlisted for the 2023 Ngaio Marsh Awards for Best Crime Novel.

www.ingramcontent.com/pod-product-compliance
Lightning Source LLC
Chambersburg PA
CBHW050607190726

48283CB00007B/2312